Anthony Ferner

Winegarden

Holland Park Press London

Published by Holland Park Press 2015

A CIP catalogue record for this book is available from The British Library.

ISBN 978-1-907320-50-7

Cover designed by Reactive Graphics

Printed and bound by
CPI Group (UK) Ltd, Croydon CR0 4YY

www.hollandparkpress.co.uk

Winegarden recounts episodes in the life of Jacob Winegarden, an agnostic Jewish professor of theoretical physics whose speciality is 'thought experimentation'.

A burly, vague, distracted man, a fan of popular films such as *Toy Story* and *Fantastic Voyage*, Jacob is still forlornly infatuated with his enigmatic wife, Miriam. She brings him back to reality: he is in a world of his own, she says, but there are things that need doing in this one.

Moving backwards and forwards in time, the book touches on different parts of Winegarden's life and thoughts, and tells a larger personal story of grief and survival, the ambivalence and persistence of love, and the meaning of being Jewish.

For Diana, Dan, Joe

THE CAT IT IS THAT DIES, PERHAPS

Professor Winegarden put his hand on the knob of the bedroom door and waited, uncertain, in the early morning light. The daily ritual, the barely resolvable daily choice: should he go back in to glimpse his wife again before he left, or not? If he did, would she wake or stay sleeping? Were she to wake, would she be irritable, saying, for example, 'For goodness' sake, Jacob, are you a child?' in that restrained murmur that made it all the more cutting. This would be painful to him. And, at the same time, like a welcome pinprick of feeling in a numb limb. But then again, she might smile sweetly and say, 'Jacob? Is that you, darling? I hope the day goes well.'

If he chose not to go in, to remain in ignorance as to whether she would wake or stay sleeping, he could speculate then on infinite possibilities, and some of these would not carry the heavy charge of loss and diminishment.

And so he held back, a burly man with thinning hair and entropic eyebrows, until some small electrical twitch of muscle led him to turn and tread down the stairs with a sigh. He would phone her later to tell her that he'd been called into the office first thing. He imagined her reproachful voice: 'On a *Saturday*? Is it that important? Are we to be ships in the night, Jacob?'

To which he would reply, 'Miriam, darling, there's been a problem.'

A problem with the experimental cat.

Winegarden came out of the drive, glanced at the icy splendour of St Augustine's church, a fixed reference point in an unpredictable world, and turned south. He strode down the tree-lined street, past the detached red-brick houses with their self-important chimneys, dwellings fit for the professoriate. At the lights he crossed over and turned right into Norfolk Road. He could walk to his office in thirty minutes, along streets whose generous sycamores

9

and copper beeches shaded him from the sun and kept him moderately dry on rainy days.

As he crossed the Harborne Road by the Bluecoat School, he recalled, as he often did at this spot, the four years in the 1990s when he'd worked in temporary accommodation nearby. While their offices were being refurbished, the research group in non-empirical experimentation had been displaced from the Poynting Building and had settled into cramped rooms above the Harborne branch of the Cats Protection League.

Though Winegarden was never sure why the location had been chosen by the hierarchs at the School of Theoretical Physics, the decision was felicitous. For the one constant in non-empirical experimentation, apart from pencil and paper, was the presence of a cat. Or at least the idea of a cat.

The manager of the Cats Protection League, perhaps as a joke, perhaps because of a problem with vermin, had lent the thought-experimenters a black cat so sleek it sometimes looked pearlescent grey. It served very well, prompting experimental thoughts and catching small rodents. While the scientists toyed with the former, the cat toyed with the latter and laid them out in neat ranks under Winegarden's desk. When the cat died, another was provided. It proved unexpectedly difficult to devise a test to falsify the hypothesis that an actual cat aided thought experiments. In the absence of which falsification, the convention continued, even after the research group's return to the Poynting Building.

This building, square and red-brick, was named after John Henry Poynting, an early professor of physics at the university. Poynting was an out-and-out empiricist who measured knowable unknowns (as Winegarden put it, before Rumsfeld), rather than the known unknowables of the quantum thought experiments conducted by Winegarden's group. Poynting, the son of a nonconformist minister, was famous for weighing the earth, and something more

10

definitive and as little open to doubt was hard to imagine. But then Poynting also believed in the 'luminiferous ether', and in God – and these signs of human frailty softened Winegarden towards him.

Jacob Winegarden, despite being a non-religious Jew, an agnostic in every vibrating atom (because being agnostic was to admit to the probable impossibility of knowing), often wondered about the existence of God. What if God both did and did not exist, or sometimes did and sometimes did not? What if He-She-It was only forced into existence – or blocked from coming into being – by thoughts and intentions in the hearts and minds of men? Or indeed women? John Henry Poynting was by upbringing a Unitarian, a denier of the Holy Trinity and hence a believer in the One God. That left too little room for equivocation. At least, thought Winegarden, the Trinity allowed for the idea that God was the Father, and at the same time the Son, and the Holy Spirit, *the pneuma*, the divine breath that was immanent in this world and in human beings.

'The breath of God.' An idea – thought the professor as he made his way along the wide grass verge of Somerset Road with its lavender-scented air – an idea that was rich in arcane possibilities, even for an agnostic. He had no time for that Dawkins character and his confident atheism. How absurd to insist that one must not believe in God. How black and white, how categorical. Winegarden smiled to himself and his eyebrows quivered in grim pleasure at the image of the man Dawkins standing on a street corner with an armful of newspapers, in the fashion of old Socialist Worker stalwarts, crying, *'Militant Atheist! Militant Atheist!'* Things were always more complicated.

Except, rarely, when they were not. When all the spins and orbits of the world's electrons aligned in such a way as to make the improbable likely, to make the incredible happen.

And at such moments, things could become very simple and you could hold in your hand the key to future states of being. Or of non-being. So, in April 1936, Winegarden's grandfather, Heinz-Josef Weingarten, cut through the hubbub of the times and recognised an instant of crystalline simplicity. He decided against the wishes of his relatives and friends to abandon familial ease, pay the Reich flight tax, and leave Germany's murderous certainties for ever. He took with him his heavily lamenting wife and their teenage son Harry – who was to become Jacob's father – and they found refuge first in Belgium and then in England.

The Weingartens lived in London for a few months, changed their name to Winegarden, established contact with the *Yekkes* of Birmingham and, joining the influx of German Jewish refugees in the city, rented a modest apartment in a bulging tenement block off Sherlock Street. By the seventies, Harry was prospering as a seller of rare books and had moved his young wife, Ruth, and Jacob, their only child, out to Edgbaston.

As he hastened now beneath the shady Spanish chestnuts of Pritchatt's Road, Jacob Winegarden remembered that the family had once had a black cat called Ganef. On a Friday night it would jump on the table and rasp away at the salty surface of the smoked salmon, laid out for the Shabbes meal, until his mother chased it away, crying, 'I'm going to kill this *farshtinkener* cat one of these days.' The cat would raise its handsome triangular head and regard her coolly before taking a final defiant lick and removing itself to a place of safety.

In his teenage years, Jacob would walk with his father the two miles to the Singers Hill Shul on Shabbes and sit in the high-backed pews, marvelling at the splendour of the white and gilt ceiling. His gaze would be drawn from his prayer book to the balcony where the women sat, and it would lock with the magnificent pale grey eyes of the Rosen girl, Miriam. Years later, having moved away, he'd meet her again at a party in Moseley and, by a miraculous conjunction of subatomic particles, he would successfully woo her.

For a year or two, around the time of his barmitzvah, Jacob became part of Rabbi Jonathan's circle of promising young men who would sit and study the Talmud on a Saturday evening in the flickering moments between Shabbes and not-Shabbes, waiting hungrily for the post-dusk meal of chopped liver and *heimische* cucumbers and *chollah*, watching the late sun stream through the windows to cast a reddish glow on the bare tables and the concentrated faces of the scholars.

The young Winegarden loved the provisionality of the Talmud, the sense of infinite exegetical shades of meaning, in which the phrases that sang out to him and entranced him were 'on the one hand ... on the other hand', and 'but then again', and 'perhaps, perhaps'. He relished the intricate twisting logic used to examine the scripture. *On the one hand,* some argued, the Torah was a creation without blemish; *on the other hand,* rival scholars would argue equally persuasively, there was much redundancy and contradiction in the Torah because it needed to reflect the redundancies and contradictions of life.

One day, the rabbi drew Jacob aside and asked if he, a young man of intellectual rigour and moral seriousness, would consider going to the Gateshead Yeshiva to train for the rabbinate. Jacob shrugged. 'Perhaps you will think about it,' said the rabbi, and Jacob said, 'Yes, perhaps,' sensing even at that age, with the eyes of Miriam Rosen haunting his dreams, that it was time to move on before other futures became foreclosed.

Professor Winegarden left the road and walked across the university athletics field, his shoes leaving grey-green imprints in the dewy grass. Looking back, he thought, all this Talmudic exploration had been the intellectual grounding for his life of non-empirical experimentation. But, as he reached the careful lawns of the campus, in the sharply angled sunlight of this June morning, reveries about the past faded away.

The dark furrows of his forehead deepened.

Whenever a problem arose with the cat, there were no easy solutions. Over the years, he and his colleagues had resigned themselves to being called the 'thought experiment people' in the popular press, and he had evolved a tight smile of forbearance should non-scientists – journalists, for example – ask questions about Schrödinger with that characteristically self-satisfied yet hesitant arching of their eyebrows. 'It's not really about Schrödinger,' Winegarden would say. 'Schrödinger was merely dipping in the common pool of tradition. But yes, a cat, it should be a cat.' And Winegarden, like a rabbi with a dull student, would patiently explain.

A typical thought experiment, he would say, might be the following: a man on a motorbike rides the Aston expressway carrying a black cat in a closed fibreglass pannier. At some point an oncoming lorry bursts across the kibbled surface of the central reservation and forces the bike head-on into the concrete side wall. Most likely the motorcyclist is killed instantly. But what of the cat, in its pannier? Does the fate of the cat depend on the intention of the lorry driver, or is it independent of it? What if the lorry driver (assuming he is a man of faith and not Richard Dawkins, for example) has prayed fervently in the infinitesimal, never-ending moment before impact? And what hidden causal mechanisms at the level of medium-sized objects such as lorries, drivers and motorcycles, or at the subatomic level of muons, gluons and bosons, might influence the fate of the cat? A relaxed but intense focus on this question might yield unexpected insights. But equally, as is the way of these things, it could prove fruitless. And the journalist from the *Birmingham Post*, or wherever, would nod with glazed incomprehension and move on.

As Winegarden swiped his card at the entrance to the Physics Department, beneath the irrefutable mass of the university clock tower, he thought of Miriam. Possibly she was still lying in bed, as she often did until late on Saturday mornings. Or perhaps she was now up and drinking a slow cup of coffee with a slight tremor in her hand. His wife had grown skinny. The light of her grey eyes had dimmed, and the cracked remains of her once plump lips were like beautiful ruins. He tried to focus on the cat, but he could think only of Miriam, and was tormented by not knowing whether he depended more on her than she depended on him, and whether this amounted to love – whatever love might be. He felt a longing, not for her as she now was, but for how, in his memory, she used to be. Miriam was a woman unconcerned by religious faith, or doubt, or uncertainty. She did not care. She had abandoned the orthodoxy of her Jewish upbringing without misgivings, retaining little but a fondness for its Baltic-tinged cuisine. In the early days of their marriage, the marine lubriciousness of schmaltz herring and gefilte fish and smoked salmon would send the two of them scurrying upstairs, giggling like teenagers, to mingle their salty bodily fluids. She would be uncomplicated in her pleasure. But he was more ambivalent. He was wary of orgasm because it represented an unambiguous end point, an undesired certainty, and he would lie back afterwards with profound melancholy and sigh.

And Miriam would ask, with the hint of a smile, 'What's wrong, darling? Is it post-coital tristesse?'

And he'd nod and say, 'Yes, PCT, perhaps, maybe,' and would wish at such moments, vaguely, that he smoked.

And then the cat clawed its way back into his consciousness. He had been woken before seven o'clock by the ringing of the telephone and, still fuddled with sleep, had lifted the receiver to hear the voice of his colleague, Dr Janet Simpson. Working into the small hours, she'd been disturbed by a terrible screeching. It was coming from his office, from the locked and windowless 'inner sanctum', as Winegarden called it, where files were kept: all the intellectual property of twenty-three years of thought experimentation. The screeches were followed by a ferocious knocking, and then by feline squeals and

15

yammerings of pain and anger. 'Perhaps,' Simpson had said, 'we – you – have been pushing that animal a bit hard …' and she'd let the note of accusation die away into silence.

As he climbed the stairs to the third floor, Winegarden was filled with dread. He entered his office and made his way to the locked door of the inner room. All was quiet. He hesitated, key in hand – he had the only key. He imagined the cat was dead. He imagined the cat was alive, and he imagined the superposition of these two states. He imagined that Janet Simpson was dreaming or mistaken. Or that the cat had slunk through a half-open window and onto the flat roof, to be joined by another. A memory slipped into his mind, unbidden and unwelcome, of the perma-tanned young woman who had lived above the baker's next to the Cats Protection League, with the tattoo at the small of her firm-skinned back, yowling her illicit passion through the partition walls on weekday afternoons when her husband was at work.

Winegarden took a deep breath to ease that beckoning tattoo from his mind. He considered again the lock and the key. Would his unlocking of the door provoke the animal's death? Or its continued existence? At what point would he, a medium-sized object, make contact with the subatomic realm and change the conjunction of particles? He puffed out his cheeks and twiddled the key between his fingers. He was disconcerted by the prospect of putting an end to uncertainty, of making a choice. Most people, when asked, hated the anxiety of not knowing, but he hated the anxiety of knowing. His heart was beating against the barrel of his chest. This was hard. He could walk away; Janet Simpson had gone home and he was alone. But he thought of Miriam and, for her, he wished to be brave.

He put the key in the lock, turned it and pushed the door into the blackness of the room.

A dark shape snaked against his leg with an accusatory miaow and disappeared along the corridor in a pattering run, its tail lifted high. Winegarden sat down at his desk and held his head in his hands, waiting for his heartbeat to slow. One never knew, one never knew. Until one did. Every decision brought a surfeit of certainty. He rose slowly from the desk, rubbing his chest to ease the lingering tightness there, and walked from the office.

He stepped out of the shadow of the Poynting Building into the heat of the sun. He glanced upwards at the vertiginous brick of the clock tower. Would a cat falling from the top, he wondered, have a chance of righting itself by the time it hit the ground? And, as it fell, would its whole life flash before it – its playful kittenhood, its furtive cleansing of flesh from discarded herring bones, its first brutal matings on a midnight lawn? Winegarden sighed deeply. It was mid-morning and the sun had dried the dew so that his shoes left no traces on the grass. He walked across the green and onto the athletics field and, feeling all of a sudden drained of energy, he traced a meandering line to Pritchatt's Road and headed north-north-west in the direction of home.

***

Jacob Winegarden climbs the stairs and stops outside the bedroom. It is eleven o'clock, but Miriam is not drinking coffee at the kitchen table, nor is she bending over the pungent roses in the south-facing flower beds. She is still in bed, asleep, or awake. Now he will be brave. He knows his bravery will alter the way atoms and the particles of atoms interact and this will change the behaviour of medium-sized bodies, like wives, for example. He lays his fingers on the door knob. He hesitates, contemplating the back of his hand, the finely wrinkled skin like tide-rippled sand and the pale brown spots and the veins glinting in the bluish light filtering into the corridor from the high round window. It is a moment containing all possibilities, of being and not-being. He turns the knob and goes in.

17

Miriam lies on her back, her chest rising and falling gently. He watches her, listens for the gentle puttering out-breath. She wakes and raises her sleep-sodden head from the pillow and frowns. She mutters, 'Jacob? What sort of time do you call this?' And then immediately she smiles, gives a feline shudder of pleasure and murmurs, 'Well, hello you, hhhmm, where have you been, come back to bed.'

The sleepy warmth of her voice saddens him with memories, or the ghostly trace of memories, of their younger selves. Is *this* love, he wonders, this constant knowing and not knowing? He sighs with a resignation that is almost contentment, and he treads softly, wearily, towards her.

Holy Moly

Jacob Winegarden, in his mid-grey marriage suit, stands on one leg. He is waiting to crash his foot down on the wrapped glass, waiting an eternity. Miriam looks at him with her pale eyes. She wants him to do it, to participate in a ceremony of centuries, to be part of the flow of time and particles. But even while wanting, she is detached, an observer, with a faint ironic smile only he can see through her white veil. It is an instant he cannot bear to leave, this heron-like, one-legged moment, because to shatter the glass is to take a step that is irreversible in space-time. And that of course, he knows, is the point of the ritual. He looks at those faces around him frozen in expectant expressions, hovering on the edge of puzzlement. Rabbi Guttmann frowns a little. Do it, thinks Jacob. Do it now. The foot descends, makes contact, breaks molecular bonds, crushes crystal lattices, rearranges atoms in space and time. The glass is shattered, the moment too. There are choruses of *mazeltov,* and *sh'koich,* and *l'chayim,* and then a bellowing cry …

***

'Professor?' inquired a student, a pale young woman in a blouse too primary for her complexion. 'Do we include the islands?'

The question seemed to come to Winegarden from a far place. 'What islands?' He recovered himself. 'Ah yes. The islands – Skye, Benbecula, that sort of thing? Yes. As you like.'

He'd hit his class of second years with a difficult question: 'And how long is the coastline of Britain?'

Incomprehension. Silence. Then, some tentative suggestions. He listened, his arms folded, smiling at the wrongness of their answers. 'Now,' he said, holding up his hand for attention, 'it all depends on the measurement scale. The smaller the ruler, the longer the coastline.'

The class stared at him, flummoxed, until – to his intense pleasure – the pale student asked, eyes wide with abrupt intellectual enlightenment, 'Is that fractals and stuff?'

'Fractals, yes. Very good.'

'And does that mean,' she went on, her eyes gleaming, 'that if the ruler is infinitely small, the coastline is infinitely long?'

Winegarden beamed at her. 'Quite so!' And he paused before adding, 'But can the scale be infinitely small in actuality, hmm?'

The student sat and tapped her teeth with the end of a pencil, considering the mysteries of the universe.

Winegarden was interested in infinity because he believed it to be the key to the world of subatomic particles, his domain. Many years later, he sneaked off one Saturday afternoon, leaving Miriam in the garden with her secateurs, and walked to the cinema on Station Road – the Jacey, he always knew it as, even when it was called something else entirely. He sat close to the screen and watched *Toy Story*, exulting in the arcane hinterland that the film opened up for him alone: 'To infinity and beyond!' he thought as he came out into the light of day.

Soon after, Miriam and he went to tea on the lawn at the house of her cousin Estelle in King's Heath. *Toy Story* was the subject of conversation. Estelle's precocious son Benjamin commented in Winegarden's hearing that Buzz Lightyear must be infinitely stupid as there was nothing 'beyond infinity'. To which Winegarden responded, in a voice so resonant and deep it cut through the chatter, 'There you are wrong. For was it not the great Georg Cantor, Benjamin, who posed the question, "How big is infinity?", and the simpletons answered, "Infinite!" And Cantor said, "You know nothing," confounding them

20

with his proof that there are many infinities and some are beyond others. As Buzz Lightyear knew.'

The lad was blushing with mortification. His mother said, 'Yes, anyway, that's all very well, Uncle Jacob's gone off on one. More cake anybody?' – she had the impatient practicality of the Rosen side of the family.

As they were driving back to their house in Edgbaston, Winegarden tried to explain the ideas to Miriam. She simply said, 'Why all this fuss with infinity? You are finite, I am finite.' That's all there is to know,' and Winegarden felt a discomfort that he tried to ward off with mental calculations and thought experiments involving half-mirrored glass and cunningly knowing particles of light, and cats concealed in boxes, and zombies ...

***

Jacob and Miriam had met as children still, at the Singers Hill Synagogue. He'd first become aware of her when, gazing up between the ivory-painted columns at the women's gallery, he saw her looking down at him. Or was it after the Shabbes service, across the laden Kiddush table, the younger teenagers pushing through the throng to knock back tiny tumblers of sweet Palwin Kiddush wine, and gobble glutinous schmaltz herring on *chollah* bread? Or in one of those interminable Sunday school classes on the Torah, where the only relief from the tedium (but what blessed relief!) was to tickle the nape of the neck of the member of the opposite sex at the desk in front of you and see them squirm with delight? Wherever it was, Winegarden still remembered the overwhelming sense that beams of agitated photons were passing between his eyes and Miriam's.

And then, nothing.

He was too shy to approach her, she too haughty to break the ice. A pattern was established, and he could not free himself from the bonds of his teenage timorousness.

But one afternoon after school, when he was helping in his father's bookshop and particles of dust drifted in Brownian motion in shafts of sunlight between the shelves, the door opened and Miriam entered. Her lips parted in surprise at the sight of him. 'Oh,' she said, 'it's you. Hello.'

And all he could think of to say, or stammer, was, 'What are you d-doing here?'

'I'm just browsing, if that's all right.'

So she looked at the shelves, and in a while they started to talk about books, and poetry. Or rather, she talked and he gabbled. He was worried his sweet, irascible father would walk in and demand to know why he was neglecting his duties for frivolities with a girl. 'Jacob, Jacob,' he imagined his father complaining in his high reproachful tone, 'a bookshop is a temple, and you are the temple servant. Not some gigolo at a party, not some lazy *lobbes*. I don't want this malarkey.' His father spoke in the over-elaborate cadences of the grateful immigrant.

Jacob showed Miriam the old volume of the collected poems of Kipling, mildewed and dog-eared, that he often took down and read lying on the wooden floorboards with his head propped up on one hand. She said, 'That's pretty old-fashioned, I prefer modern stuff. Ted Hughes, that sort of thing.' She sounded much older than her fifteen years. And she added, as if to soothe his ego, 'But I really liked the Just-So Stories, when I was a girl. The Cat that Walked by Itself, especially. Have you read *The Bell Jar,* by the way? Sylvia Plath?'

Jacob did not like to admit that he'd never heard of Ted Hughes or Sylvia Plath. Miriam said, 'She bit his cheek, Ted Hughes's I mean, when they first met. She drew blood, you know.'

He coloured: the disturbing thought was in his mind that he'd very much like Miriam to bite his cheek and draw blood. But she did not. She did something more shocking. She announced that she was looking for a book to read on a journey, as her family were moving to London at the end of the week. Leaving Birmingham. Going. For good.

Later, Winegarden could only remember leaning against the bookshelves, shocked speechless, feeling she'd stabbed him in the heart. He was like a zombie as he took her money for a Penguin volume of short stories by Katherine Mansfield and *The Intelligent Woman's Guide to Atomic Radiation*, and was scarcely aware that she'd leant over and grazed his cheek – with her lips, not her teeth – before walking out of the shop and out of his life. He caught the fresh but heady whiff of her. It would be nearly five years before they saw each other again.

It was around this time that, encouraged by his teachers, Jacob started to grasp the truths of quantum mechanics. One day, hunting through the storeroom of his father's shop in search of possible erotica, his fumbling hands opened a box stashed behind a bookcase, and his hands trembled even more to discover, not slim books with interestingly frank engravings, but several ancient volumes of *Annalen der Physik*. Sneezing from the dust on the pages, he quite forgot his original quest. Soon, with his schoolboy German and a dictionary, he was edging his way through some of the great ideas of twentieth-century science; and understanding but a small portion of what he read.

He gasped in awe as the mysteries of superposition slowly dawned on him: that a particle may exist in all its theoretical states of being, and does in fact exist in all those states at once – until it is observed. He relished the uncertainty at the heart of quantum theory, he was thrilled by the notion of quantum tunnelling. And he loved the idea of quantum entanglement because it explained what he felt for Miriam. He had a strong sense that she was, in some real way, ever-present, that he and she were somehow tied together. Two subatomic particles, once linked by energy and momentum, remain entangled, even when separated by tracts of space-time. Whatever state the one is in, the other will be in a corresponding state. He read that Einstein had hated the notion, calling it 'spooky action at a distance', yet theory and experiments proved it to be so. For Jacob, it was a small leap to think in terms of the quantum entanglement of large bodies. This softened the blow of separation, and gave him a ridiculous kind of hope.

***

Winegarden and Miriam met again at a garden party in Moseley. They were both in their first year of university. She was in skittish mood, saying, 'Well! Are you going to ask me what I'm doing here? Like you did last time you saw me.' She laughed.

Jacob pretended not to remember. He was less tongue-tied and timid, a little more experienced with women. A certain kind of female took to his bulky ursine presence and his shy grin and his deep-voiced gentleness. There was something absent and other-worldly about him, and some women liked that too.

'Have you been doing interesting things?' she asked him, with the usual trace of ironic amusement in her voice. To him, she was very beautiful.

'Well, perhaps not interesting to you, but to me interesting, yes. I've been exploring incredibly small things and incredibly large things ...'

'What, like microbes and whales, I suppose?'

'More like electrons and galaxies. And you can't understand one without the other.'

She looked at him with her magnetic grey eyes, and he felt hollow inside, as if all the tubing and pipework of his body were empty, with a dipping sensation like on fairground rides.

'And what about the world we actually live in?' she said. 'Do you do anything in this world at all?'

'Hmmm. The cinema, I suppose. Did you see *Fantastic Voyage*?'

They talked about films, and books, and the courses they were doing, and they found that they were both in residences of the University of London, quite close to each other.

'You'll visit me in London,' she said as they parted, omitting to say where she lived, perhaps to test his perseverance. He found her parents' telephone number from directory enquiries, and her intimidating father interrogated him in a fierce German accent until Jacob had the sense to mention his surname. 'Winegarden as in Weingarten?!' asked Mr Rosen. 'Of Moseley? Harry Weingarten your father? Why didn't you say so before!' He dictated his daughter's address to Jacob, with the final injunction that there would be 'no funny business, no hanky-panky, you got that?'

And a couple of weeks later, Jacob was walking through the dark oak-panelled corridors of the female students' hall of residence. He sat on the wooden chair in Miriam's tiny cell of a room which was painted in a morose shade of yellow ochre. She perched on the bed, as demure and fragile as a silver birch. He felt ill-at-ease. The swinging sixties were passing him by, he did not know how to behave, or what was expected of him. He spent his days, and often much of his nights, in laboratories. While his peers were out partying, he was studying.

He'd brought Miriam a present of smoked salmon bagels from Grodzinski's. She smiled and set the package aside. She seemed so distant, unreachable, sitting on the bed with her legs tucked up beneath her.

'We're supposed to keep the door open,' she said.

'Oh.'

'But rules like that are stupid I think, don't you?'

'I suppose ...'

She stared at him with her luminous eyes. He was aware of a change in the atmosphere. The atoms had rearranged themselves in the room; it felt the same, yet charged. He did not know what was happening, his universe was stalling, falling.

Somehow he knew that he must rise from the chair and sit beside her on the bed, and put his arm around her shoulder. She turned towards him.

'We're supposed to have kept one foot on the floor!' she laughed. 'That's what the rules say.'

'Perhaps, if the rules say, we'd better ...'

He thought, you can bite my cheek if you want.

She said, 'Don't be silly,' and took his hand and pulled it to her breast.

Jacob felt the live, delicately dangerous thing fluttering under his fingers. He was flustered and began to shiver. But she smiled. 'Let's break more rules.' She pulled her cotton blouse over her head, with a cross-armed agility that surprised him, and his heart was beating so fiercely he dared not, could not, say a word.

Her breasts were not globes, but more like elongated party balloons, firm and elastic and buoyant with their dark aureoles and thick nipples.

She was kissing him. He tasted the salt on her lips and then her tongue, and was seized by a mad vertigo of excitement and panic. They kissed and pawed at each other, and she bit his shoulder and licked his face, and then she pulled him to her with unexpected force. Winegarden considered at the edge of his mind the superposition of bodies and the entanglement of limbs and the tunnelling of weak flesh through matter, and of a host of excited particles contained in a spurting wave, and he could no longer hold himself back. Time did not stand still, it went forwards and it reversed, and he was alive and he was dead.

Afterwards, the entropy of his world had tended to a maximum and there was an intoxicating aroma of forbidden rock pools, and witch hazel, and the steam that rises from the cracking shells of roasted chestnuts, and then ... he lay back filled with a profound melancholy that she stroked away with her warm, firm little hand.

'Oh God, I'm sorry,' he stammered, 'I shouldn't have … I should have asked if …'

'It's all right,' she said, 'I'm on the pill.'

He went cold, a small tear opening in the fabric of his briefly joyful universe: she had a past, and it did not include him. And if she had a past, perhaps she'd have a future, also without him.

In years to come, he would have to adjust to the uncertainty of not knowing. If she were to become pregnant, would he be the father, or merely the cuckolded husband? He decided to follow the principles of quantum physics, and be both cuckolded and, superposed, uncuckolded. Ascertaining the fact of the matter would destroy uncertainty, and with it, peace of mind. For years he would distract himself from this pain by engaging in sterile thought experiments in which he imagined making love to another woman. They always enmeshed him in contradiction and paradox to do with love and desire, and he realised that such an act would be impossible for him.

One day, not long after they were married, when Miriam came home much later than she'd told him she would, his self-control faltered and he could not prevent himself from asking her where she'd been, and why she was so late home. She gave him her haughty look.

'Is this an interrogation?'

'Surely I have a right to know, Miriam. I am your husband.'

She said as if correcting a misguided child, 'You have a right to ask, Jacob, but not a right to know.'

'But …'

'No buts. You are married to me, you do not own me. I am not a possession.'

He shook his head, appalled. 'Why can we not talk even?'

'This is not being feminist, Jacob, this is being human,' she said, at a knight's move to his question. 'The human that *I* am. Which is one with places in my heart and mind that you do not have access to.'

This unknowableness hurt Winegarden, but it also fuelled his love for her, and his theoretical speculations. It made him think differently about the future and time, and also about the taboo things, those things that science was supposed to shun: love, and the pain of loving, grief, desire, the soul, the transcendent. How could it all be arranged and ordered into one unified physics? But then, he reflected, too much tidiness, too much order, led to the tidying away of human beings. In mental asylums, or old age homes, in prisons, or in gas chambers. So, as ever it was a balance. On the one hand ... on the other hand. And even Miriam's caressing fingers could not ease these thoughts from his mind.

***

The glass is smashed and the celebrants are shouting *mazeltov,* and *sh'koich,* and there are cheers, and Jacob's father rises up with a face of great anger, and he bellows, 'No! Joy must be tempered by sadness! This shattered glass is a reminder that life is not a *fairy* tale.' He has fled the Nazis and survived.

"'If I forget you, O Jerusalem",' he roars in his still German-accented English, '"let my right hand lose its cunning, let my tongue cleave to the roof of my mouth!"'

The congregants are stunned into silence. Their eyes are on him. He says, shaking his leonine head, *'Ayd, noshir es shir Adonoi, ul udmus naichor*! "How shall we sing the Lord's song in a foreign land?"' His guttural mittel-European 'r's' growl at the back of his throat.

Miriam's smile has faded and she has turned pale. In the confusion the napkin in which the glass was wrapped has burst its seams, and shards have escaped onto the floor of the synagogue. And for some reason, possibly as a reflex, Miriam gathers her wedding gown to her knees and stoops and picks up a sliver, and cuts herself. Winegarden thinks, 'With this blood I thee wed', and wishes to take her fingers to his mouth and kiss them.

But of course he does not.

Instead he recalls the scene of an hour earlier when Rabbi Hirsch Guttmann takes Jacob and Miriam into a side room, with pictures of past rabbis on the walls. Rabbi Guttmann is a tubby man, slightly boss-eyed. He smiles and speaks kindly and elliptically about marriage and their duties one to another. Then his face turns severe and his tone is minatory and jovial at once.

'You must avoid the sin of Onan!' He is looking at Jacob with one eye and the wall with the other. 'Like the plague. Avoid. With each other, no? Enjoy! Two is better than one!' Jacob backs uncomfortably away from his gaze, not sure which eye to focus on.

'Every day! You should do it every day, the two of you!' The rabbi's accent is sort of Bronx-Birmingham. 'Thursday, at it! Friday, at it! Saturday, at it. Every day! Holy moly, the more times the merrier!'

Then his severe scowl gives way to a lovely beam of a smile, and to Jacob's surprise he's grasped a roll of Miriam's pretty cheek between two knuckles and is gently jiggling it.

'You are children, kids! Make hay while the sun shines! And when it's raining, make babies!'

He pats her. '*Mazeltov, mazeltov.* Enjoy!' and he holds out a chubby hand for them to pass out of the room …

But now, Jacob's father's angry voice brings him back to the present. 'Jacob! Jacob! Do not stand there like a *shme'gegeh*! Respond to me!'

Jacob stares at him, and feels his own anger rising.

Harry Winegarden, by nature so equable and sweet until these fierce gusts of rage blow up out of nowhere, turns full circle, eyeing the cowed congregation. People shrink from him. The rabbi is laying a hand on his arm but he shrugs it away. He declaims, fiercely, "'O daughter of Babylon, that art to be destroyed. Happy shall he be, that taketh and dasheth thy little ones against the rock! Amen.'"

Miriam's hand has gone to her face in horror.

'Enough!' shouts Jacob with a force that he does not know he possessed, 'Dad, enough!', and the man looks at him with surprise, and alarm, as if he's been startled awake from a bad dream, and at last allows himself to be led away.

Miriam is in tears. Jacob puts his arm around her. 'Let us continue,' says Rabbi Guttmann, and he smiles at the congregation as though nothing has happened.

Miriam's bleeding finger has spotted her wedding dress with scarlet. The wives of the synagogue elders quiver with superstitious disapproval. Verses of Kipling come to Winegarden's mind. 'Lo! Ere the blood-gush has ceased, forward her soul rushes … She is away to her tryst. Who is her pandar? Death!' He shudders.

The rabbi leads the congregation in the singing of a psalm. The voices are subdued, the faces hot and heavy with shock. But she, Miriam, smiles at Jacob now, and raises her voice, high and clear, *shir hamaalos, b'shuv adonai, es shives tziyon hayinu k'chol'mim*, and he feels her elbow resting gently against his side, and he swells with his love for her.

Winegarden sat in the waiting room, undignified in a hospital gown. He had been there, it seemed, for hours, alongside three others. An old woman. A middle-aged woman. An aggressive, tattooed man, much younger. Each had kept on their shoes and socks, and beside each was a transparent plastic bag of belongings, tumbled inside, like looking through the window of a washing machine. Winegarden felt stripped of his professorial status, of his individuality, reduced by this garb to the mournfully egalitarian congregation of hospital out-patients. Of those to whom things were to be done.

On the television in the corner, a TV chef soundlessly demonstrated how to bone a chicken. He had a vapid smile and unearthly white teeth; Winegarden felt a sense of unreality, of dislocation. More time passed, no one spoke.

A nurse came in and said, 'Mrs Underwood?', and the older woman rose and followed the nurse out of the room, dragging her transparent sack of clothes behind her.

Earlier, much earlier, Winegarden had sat in a nurse's office and she'd taken his blood pressure. 'My!' she said, 'it's off the scale. Your first time is it? You'll be fine when the sedative kicks in.'

'Sedative.'

'Yes,' said the nurse, inserting a needle and a plastic widget into the back of his hand and taping it in place. 'It will calm you.'

I am calm, thought Winegarden. As calm as you could be when a surgeon was about to insert a colonoscope through your anus and up your colon as far as it would go.

It was on his fifty-fifth birthday that he'd first received the package in the post. An uneven, bulky A5 envelope. A free sample, he thought. A biro from a charity. A sachet of shampoo – that would be wasted on the wiry sproutings that were his hair. Inside, there was no biro and no shampoo, but a set of instructions and a card with four little openings or portals, and four little wooden spatulas. It was for testing the excrement extruded from his ageing bowels to spot something called 'faecal occult blood'. Winegarden examined it. Ah, he thought, occult. Kabbalah. Mysticism. Not for me. And he neatly replaced the kit in its envelope and left it out of sight on the small shelf in the downstairs toilet, and forgot about it.

Until a year later, near enough to the day, a second package dropped through the letter box. Had Miriam also had one, he wondered? But it was not the sort of question Jacob Winegarden could ask his wife. The second envelope was placed beside the first, on the shelf in the downstairs toilet. But the following day, after breakfast, and through a process of decision-making driven by the random concurrence of small probabilities, Winegarden went downstairs and into the loo with a clear plastic bag. He opened the kit and lifted the card window and, having performed an act of agility, captured a smear of his own excrement with the wooden spatula and daubed it on the white square of the first opening. For the next three days, he repeated the ritual, with clumsy-fingered care and a grimace of distaste.

This close engagement with one's body's own waste products was hard for Winegarden. You could live the life of the mind all you wanted, you could lock yourself away to contemplate the tiny humming flea circus of atoms and electrons, with their spins and orbits and charges. But sooner or later you were dragged back to the human world of bodily effluvia and earthy smells and base desires. It brought to mind the Golem of Prague, the famous mud-man summoned into half-life by Rabbi Loew to protect the Jews of Eastern Europe. To protect them against the pogroms, and the blood libels, and themselves. To save them from their own passivity, their chronic lack of physicality, their inability to fight back against their tormentors. Of course, thought Winegarden that was then, before things changed. Before Jews learned how to become tormentors in their turn. But you couldn't think these things, couldn't say them, without becoming that most reviled of creatures, the 'self-hating Jew'.

'Darren Shields,' called the nurse, and the tattooed young fellow got up and followed her, jaunty and with bravado, no sedative needle in the back of his hand. He looked at Winegarden as he passed and gave a faint dip of the head, the hint of a smile, like a battle-hardened trooper going over the top. For some reason, the gesture touched Winegarden, gave him a sense of belonging.

Strange to think that there were things going on in his body that he knew nothing about. His body had acted on its own behalf, without his say-so. That's what the faecal occult blood test indicated. It had come back positive. He'd had no inkling. There was no correlate at the surface of what was happening deep within, hidden from view, in all those concealed tubes and pumps and valves and containers.

The door to the waiting room opened again and a nurse appeared. 'Mr Winegarden?' He looked at the clock: he'd been sitting there for three hours in his hospital gown, the backs of his thighs stuck to the clammy plastic of the chair.

'Would you like to come with me.'

He followed her into a small room crowded with equipment and with medical people. There was the hum and suck of machinery.

He felt out of control, he felt he was being acted upon, not acting. They prepared to attach a line to the needle in the back of his hand.

'We'll just sedate you …' began the nurse.

'No,' said Winegarden, startled by the authority in his own voice. He wasn't used to that. 'I'll do it without.'

'That's fine,' said the nurse. 'If you change your mind, we can always …'

'Thank you.'

The surgeon introduced himself: a Mr Ashok Gupta, Professor of Colorectal Surgery. The man's title reassured Winegarden; he was back among familiar people, there was a point of contact.

He lay on the bed as instructed, facing a large colour monitor attached to the wall beside him. By habit, he distracted himself with a thought experiment. What would happen if one could alter the molecular properties of the solid tissue of the human body so that light was no longer refracted but passed straight through? So that what was opaque became transparent? It might conceivably work with organic substances, there were species of crustaceans that had translucent exoskeletons. Perhaps if you could see the organs within, see their routine grindings and pumpings and osmotic perfusions, you might anticipate and prevent this betrayal of the body by the body.

Winegarden felt Professor Gupta insert the camera on its long flexible tube, the colonoscope. A wince of discomfort, then ... nothing. He watched on the monitor as the probe began its fantastic voyage. This was not so bad.

A transparent body. Hmm. You might obtain insights into the workings of the organs, the mind, the emotions. Into what it meant to be human. *Hard-hearted. Having the stomach for it. Full of bile. Has he got the guts? Choler, choleric. Black bile. Yellow bile.* Like those school-playground tongue-twisters: Peter Piper picked a peck of pickled pepper ... Red lorry, yellow lorry, red lorry, yellow lorry. Black bile, yellow bile, black bile, yellow bile.

Irritated with the random firings of his consciousness, Winegarden brought himself back to the question in hand. Some would say that feelings, emotions, beliefs, prejudices could be traced to what the body is doing, unbeknown to you, at a given moment, and are nothing more or less than those physical processes. But could you reduce feelings to electrical discharges in the brain, or secretions of chemicals in the gut, or hormones coursing through the bloodstream?

34

He felt his stomach blow up with gas.

'We're pumping in air,' said the surgeon, 'so we can see what we're doing. You may feel a little bloating.'

He watched on the monitor. A patch of his colon quivered like jelly at the approach of the probe. The picture on the screen had gone fuzzy.

'Ha, I felt that,' said the surgeon. 'Just a spasm. That's the thing about this procedure, there's no hiding place for your emotions!'

Have I got the guts, thought Winegarden. The nurse said, 'We'll just give you a little sedative to relax your insides ...'

'No,' he replied, through tight jaws. 'No sedative.'

'OK,' said Gupta a moment later, 'all quiet on the western front.'

Winegarden returned to his small thought experiment. If one could see these things happening, would it lessen the alienation from one's own self that one always felt, the unbridgeable gap between one's mind and one's body? Or would transparency merely trigger uncontrollable waves of emotion – fear, disgust, anxiety, jealousy, anger ...? If you could observe everything, you'd be watching for signs the whole time. Are those the jealousy chemicals now flooding your heart, you'd wonder, and you would think of Miriam and feel a bitter pang of jealousy; and this could become a self-reinforcing spiral.

Gupta said, 'We are approaching the top of the sigmoid colon.'

Winegarden looked up at the screen. The inner space – his inner space – was so glistening pink and *alive*, rolling and contracting before the tip of the probe. And clean as a whistle, no trace of base substance, no *faecal matter*. Living breathing tissue, an organism, quite separate from him, to which he was host. He felt an obscure pride in making its acquaintance. Mine, he thought, and I never knew.

The surgeon asked, 'Are you watching the cricket? That Jadeja, his action is a little low-slung, as it were, he needs to give the ball more air.'

No more air, thought Winegarden abstractedly, please no more air. They discussed doosras and sliders for a few moments.

Gupta said, 'Sigmoid. So-called because of its shape, like the letter sigma.'

Sigmund Freud. Sigmeud Frund. Sigmund Colon, thought Winegarden. A Sigmeudian slip. He hoped he hadn't said it aloud.

'Having gone straight up,' continued Professor Gupta, 'we venture round the bend – then in particular you may experience a little discomfort – and down to the vermiform appendix. We photograph the entrance to the small intestine, like tourists, to show that we've been, and we retreat, dealing with issues on the way.'

'Issues', thought Winegarden. Issues with tissues. Into his mind came a vision of his ten-year-old self, standing on Station Parade in Southgate outside the entrance to the Underground, the Piccadilly line, the Piccalilli line, on a visit to his cousins. He was watching a kosher butcher eviscerate chickens, and realising – and for the first time, like a revelation – that what they ate at home, warm on Friday nights to usher in the Shabbes, and cold during the week, came from a once-live creature. A creature pulsating with guts and heart and fat, like himself. This existential moment had hypnotised him into immobility outside the butcher's window.

And now he was staring at his own guts on the monitor, at last connected, integral. Time passed. It was like being in an aeroplane, the same confined stillness, the same whirring noises. Except that here it was as if they were trying to blow up his insides with gas. Like Japanese torturers of the Second World War, he thought. Feeding their victims uncooked rice and forcing water down their throats until their stomachs exploded.

As ever with Winegarden, at the periphery of his rational scientist's mind and his convoluted thought experiments was a murky zone of half-formed perceptions and half-felt emotions, and at the very edge of these lay Miriam. When he yearned for transparency, what he really hankered after was to see the inner workings of his wife. She had an unyielding opacity. The paradox was that it was this very unknowableness that drove his love for her, and his need, and his jealousy. He sensed that were she ever to become transparent to him, his love would wither. Not because of the things he saw there, merely because he could now see them.

'At nine centimetres, two small polyps. Pedunculated,' murmured the surgeon, and a nurse inscribed crosses on a diagram of the colon on her clipboard.

Ah, thought Winegarden, remembering the enticing legends on hand-drawn maps in books of fantasy and adventure that he found in his father's bookshop, 'Here be dragons'. But in truth they were more like sea anemones, waving around in his gut, rippling under the gusts of air. His body turning against itself, transforming good tissue into something else, something strange and unwelcome.

Gupta carried on his affable chat. Edgbaston cricket ground was on their doorstep, how lucky, he said.

'I rarely get time to visit,' replied Winegarden, 'my days are taken up with my work. Though a few years ago I did see the great Muralitharan, with his withered arm, his staring eyes.'

'Oh my gosh, the fearsome Murali, he was the bane of our Indian batsmen too.' He chuckled. 'And what is your line of work, Mr Winegarden?'

'I'm an, erm … an experimental physicist. At the University.'

'Experimental physics, eh. Interesting.'

'Experimental but of the non-empirical kind.'

Gupta said, 'Very good.'

'Thought experiments,' Winegarden felt obliged to clarify.

'Yes, yes. I understand. I see a value to medicine also in non-empirical experimentation. Now please, lie on your back for a moment, you may feel a little push, we're going round the upper bend. If you feel too much pressure in your gut, feel free to expel some air.' The surgeon chuckled. 'No one can hear with all the racket of the machinery, and of course there is no faecal residue to worry about. So feel free, fart away.'

Winegarden felt not free but deeply inhibited. This was not something to be done in front of strangers, or even friends, and certainly not in front of Miriam. But the pressure in his intestines was growing unbearable. He thought, 'Blessed art thou oh Lord our God, King of the Universe, who created us with many bodily openings and cavities.'

He let go, and felt a wave of self-reproach and blessed relief. 'The shame and humiliation of our lives is known to you, Oh Lord, and at our end, worms and maggots await us.'

'Interesting, interesting,' Gupta was saying, entirely unmoved by Winegarden's nether exhalations. 'What if ... What if I were to shrink down to the size of a sigmoidoscope, for example ... Or an arterioscope or an athroscope ...? I could stand on the very spot and ponder how to repair damage, how to resolve tricky biochemical problems. I could approach the blood brain barrier and contemplate the mind-body interface as a philosophico-physiological problem. Am I on the right track? Yes, hmm? Very good, very good.'

'*Fantastic Voyage,*' said Winegarden. 'It's a film. That's what they did, I saw it as a young lad, at the Jacey Film Theatre on Station Street.'

'Good. Fantastic. Was that before or after it started with the pornography?' There was a slight pause. Gupta said, 'Oh, there's something here, let's take a closer look.'

The image on the screen magnified. 'Yes, this is quite a big one. Not pedunculated like the others. Another kind of polyp. More *flat*. Sessile we call it.'

'Sessile,' repeated Winegarden, anxiety cutting through the bloated discomfort.

'Perhaps not as friendly as one would like,' said Gupta. A sessile giant, something larval and gross and spreading, like a colonic Jabba the Hut. Precursor to something viler still.

'Quite a size indeed. Fifteen millimetres at least. That will have been silently growing for ten years, maybe twenty. Nothing to feel. No symptoms. Just the trace of faecal occult blood, that is all.'

Gupta fell silent except for occasional truncated commands to his staff. Winegarden could not see the man, only the monitor, but he sensed a new tense concentration. He thought, is this what it means to be, literally, a self-hating Jew? When a part of your Jewish gut turns against itself and becomes something other, something alien and … gentile? Is it your reward for not eating kosher? For all those Spanish hams and chorizos? Those lobsters you gorged on when you had money in your pocket for the first time, as a young lecturer? And now, your body is consuming your body.

The surgeon's voice became lighter again.

'Well, here we are. Journey's end. You see? That dark opening is the small intestine. Very good. The technician will take a still photo. You can upload it to Facebook if you wish.'

'Perhaps not.'

'OK,' Gupta continued, 'so we turn round and we come back, and we do what we have to do.'

There was a long withdrawing of apparatus from the hollow tube of the colonoscope, the insertion of other apparatus. On the screen, the micro-tool emerged from the probe. A loop of wire, like a noose. The pedunculated

39

polyps were hooked, the noose was tightened. They each suffered strangulation, followed by extirpation. The unanchored growths were now flushed down the colon, like eels swimming towards the sea.

'We attach a kind of net to the bottom of the 'scope,' said Gupta, 'and we fish them out at the egress.'

The catch was quickly bundled into a plastic tub and capped and labelled for the analysts. 'And now,' said the surgeon, 'for the big fellow.' His accent was educated, suave – a Cambridge-Delhi hybrid.

'Where are you from, actually?'

'King's Heath,' said Gupta. 'King's Heath, Delhi, Boston.'

Birmingham is the new Salonika, the new Seville, or Smyrna, thought Winegarden. Where Jews and Christians and Sikhs and Muslims rub along together and make things work. A vibrant coat of many colours. But where was the golden age of Salonika now? Or Seville? Or Vienna, he thought. Two hundred years of flourishing excellence, then darkness falls. Things work, until they do not. Will a time come again in Britain? In Birmingham? We have to be thankful that we live in a moment of respite.

The thing was like jelly fungus, with its rippled surface. 'Here we must take care. Our margin for error is small. We remove it in segments ...'

Winegarden had always assumed, by gut feeling (as it were) rather than on the basis of any evidence, whether empirical or non-empirical, that he'd die of a heart attack, or possibly a fulminating stroke. Not by the malignant treachery of a few millimetres of colon. His worldview had been shaken.

'And if you make an error?' he asked the doctor.

'We shan't make an error. However, if for the sake of argument we did, we are talking, hmm, perforated colon. Emergency surgery. Long recovery.' He paused and watched as on the screen a tiny cutting implement, like the scissors on a Swiss army knife, appeared from the end of the probe.

'But at least you're all prepped!' Gupta laughed. Winegarden winced. He had no need to be reminded of the radical purging he had undergone in the previous twenty-four hours: the contents of his guts liquefied, so it seemed, and expelled violently, like the jet from a high-pressure hose. The surgeon continued his chat, but Winegarden sensed beneath the joviality a seriousness, an urgency. The voices of the medical team – the nurses, the video technician, Gupta himself – had become tauter, more restrained.

'Snip snap with my snickersnee,' murmured the doctor as a lump of polyp was excised and flushed away. And piece by piece the monstrous growth was disassembled, dismembered alive. It was zapped with hot pulses to cauterise the wound, flushed with styptic fluids. The detritus journeyed towards the light, was netted, extricated, potted, capped and labelled.

A blue dye was injected into the site of the excision. My first tattoo, mused Winegarden, a very discreet one. So that the handiwork, explained Gupta, could be re-examined in three months' time, and duly admired, or remediated. His tone was easy again, and Winegarden felt easier too.

A big one that, and tiredness was setting in, and a certain melancholy as his thoughts returned to Miriam, her lack of transparency. He'd say to her, in the early days, 'There are so many things I don't know about you.'

'Of course. And about everybody. And me about you, Jacob. So what?'

'I mean, there are things I don't know I don't know.'

'Like what? For example?' she said. And had he been able to respond, she would have dismissed him with an airy remark, such as, 'Oh, for heaven's sake, get over it, it's not that bad.'

For her, the universe was much simpler. If Rabbi Hillel's injunction was 'do as you would be done by', Miriam's was more 'do unto, or be done unto', and she had an imperious dog owner's manner. Command or be commanded. In the first years of marriage, she would say things like, 'Jacob, hand round the nibbles to our guests,' in a tone that implied that she took compliance for granted.

Once, in front of a group of friends, he turned to her with pained eyes and hissed, 'Miriam, please. That you should speak to me in that tone of voice, I don't care for it. I'm not a dog.'

She looked at him calmly and replied, 'No darling, you're not a dog. But you are in a world of your own, and there are things that need doing in this one.'

He'd said, his choler rising, as if the guests were not there or were mere wallpaper, 'What will it be next? "Sit!" "Stay!" "Fetch!"?'

Compliance scared him. The phrase that always seeped into his mind at such moments, from the Passover service, was, 'I was once a slave in Egypt.' 'I was once a slave', not 'they were once slaves ...'. Every Jew is asked to identify with bondage. As a child, he used to ask himself, and uncomprehending adults, 'How come they never rebelled, the Jews in the camps? How come they didn't try to escape? How could they just go to their deaths, allow themselves to be gassed? Because they *knew*, didn't they?' (The Nazis, the background radiation of Winegarden's moral universe. The ultimate thought-experimentalists gone rogue.)

And the adults would brush him off, or look serious and say, 'But Jake, things are a bit more complicated in real life.' And they were right.

'Yes, fine, darling,' Miriam had responded after his outburst, and she had smiled sweetly at the guests who were making uncomfortable little half-chuckling noises. But afterwards, when the guests had gone, she'd turned on him. 'How could you say that! In front of them! How could you, they're not even Jewish!' Her eyes, untypically, were wet. 'Honestly! To say I treat you like a dog ...'

'Well,' said Winegarden, 'perhaps "dog" is a bit strong.'

'Yes! It is!'

Dogs, he reflected, hold a special revulsion for Jews, as pigs do. They are unclean, their habits are vile (they lick their openings and cavities), they are associated with German guards and death camps, and pogroms throughout the ages.

He said, 'I'm sorry darling. I suppose I meant more lapdog, rather than, say, Alsatian ...'

'I'm sorry too,' she responded. 'The last thing I want to do is *belittle* you.'

He smiled, despite himself, he with his spreading thirteen stone to her eight and a half. She kissed him and stroked his face with her small soft fingers.

Winegarden was brought back to the present by a moment of sharp discomfort, and Gupta said, 'We're all done here.'

A nurse helped Winegarden carry his bundle and brought him to a recovery ward. Professor Gupta looked in. 'Results should be through in ten days, you can phone the nurse, but I'm pretty sure we've caught things in time and there will be nothing to worry about. Well done, well done indeed, you stood up remarkably, considering.'

Winegarden gave a brief nod.

The surgeon added, 'Your system has received quite an insult.'

So it has, thought Winegarden. An insult, a humiliation. Yet he had withstood it. A cautious man, he was not physically brave or daring. This was the nearest he would have come to feeling like a warrior: battered and achingly weary, but also with an invigorating sense of fortitude, of having crossed the mine-strewn wasteland and survived.

Gupta said, 'Any kids, Mr Winegarden?'

Winegarden was silent, his mouth half-opened as if surprised.

'I ask,' added Gupta, 'because genetic testing might be worthwhile. Precautionary principle. You know, these things can be hereditary ... Anyhow, talk to your GP.'

43

Belatedly, Winegarden murmured, 'No, no children.'

If he had a son, he thought, that son would be in his thirties now. In a career. Or, having lost his way somehow, unemployed; or stacking shelves. Well or ill. Content or melancholic. With children of his own. Or not.

With future prospects of bowel disease.

Spared all that of course, spared all that.

***

That night, ill and feverish, he slept only in short shallow bursts and woke each time disorientated, with a deep malaise. He was startled by a knock at the door. The postman stood in front of him holding a letter. 'Mr Jacob Winegarden?'

'Professor Winegarden. Yes?'

'It's your test results,' said the postman.

'How would you know?' Winegarden's voice had turned frosty.

'Because it's a see-through letter.'

'Ah, I see. And what does it say?'

'It's positive.'

'Hmm. Positive in the sense that it's a positive test for malignant cells? Or positive in the sense that it's positive news?'

'Yes,' said the postman.

Winegarden awoke then, the sweat drying on his forehead, and he put out his hand and felt for Miriam's shoulder, warm and gently rising and falling, and was momentarily reassured that he could deal with what the future held for him and for the guts within him.

'Let's face it Prof, we're not going anywhere,' said Bad Bob, 'other than feet first.' He leant in close, and took hold of the back of Winegarden's chair, his knuckles knobbly.

'Perhaps,' said Winegarden. It was unclear to him why he was in this place of confinement, with its over-lit rooms, orderlies in navy polyester uniforms, the odour of ageing humans. Possibly it was that business with his hands around her neck? He'd held his hands around her neck. Had he not? He imagined the fingers squeezing and closing in on themselves as they encompassed the shrunken flesh of her. Poor Miriam. He couldn't remember now why it had been necessary.

Feet first, hmm. Winegarden, a man in love with ambivalence and uncertainty, was intrigued by the possibilities of death. You had your Christian notions of resurrection, for example. Or you had zombies, brought back to a half-life by Haitian sorcerers. Zombies were perfect subjects for non-empirical experimentation. At one time he'd even imagined that they might replace cats, since they embodied states of being and not being. A zombie is on the borderland between life and death. Extradition proceedings have commenced but have become bogged down. Did zombies have souls, he wondered. And what would happen to his own soul at the actual point of death, would it depart his body with, as Rabbi Feinstein says, a sharp metaphysical pain? Or was it slipping away even now, like a shy stranger at a party? He was sure he'd had a well-worked-out view on all this, as a younger man.

'What is it again you were a professor of, Prof?' asked Bad Bob. It was not remembered how he'd come by his name.

'Physics,' said Winegarden. 'At the University. Non-empirical experimentation, pencil and paper stuff, generally involving cats. About cats being somehow there and not there. Occasionally zombies. Or Golems.'

'Zombies, eh? Cats, eh?' said Bad Bob. 'Like Macavity, always defying gravity. And when they reach the scene of crime … That the sort of thing you mean?'

'Well, in a way.'

Zombification, explained Winegarden, was probably caused by catatonic schizophrenia, or by damage to the basal ganglia, or by …

'I thought you were a physicist, not a ruddy brain surgeon.'

'You need to know a bit of physiology if you're going to do experiments on cats.'

'Experiments? Vivisection!? I hope to goodness those animal liberation …'

'No,' interrupted Winegarden, 'not vivisection. As I said, or implied, thought experiments.'

'I get you. You brainwash the poor soddin' cats.'

'No, Bob. Thoughts in your mind, not in the cat's mind. It's … It's hard to explain.' It was hard to explain, and when he tried to remember how it used to be done, it was muzzy.

'Always land on their feet, cats, don't they?' A gleam came into Bad Bob's eye. 'OK Prof, here's a little thought experiment for you. How about … how about if you took a cat, yeah, and strapped a piece of buttered toast to its back, *buttered side up*. And then, you chuck it out the flaming window, right. OK, so the question is …'

Winegarden tightened his eyebrows, once inky black, now quite white. 'I see your point, Bob.'

'Exactly! Can't land on its feet, 'cause the toast would be buttered side up, and that can't happen as it blatantly violates Sod's Law. And it can't land on its back 'cause cats always land on …'

'I get it,' said Winegarden wearily.

One of the orderlies, or warders, came round the room with pots of tea. She was young and tall, and black. She was too … benevolent-looking, thought Winegarden. He felt cheated, as if his crime deserved harsher treatment.

'A refill, Professor?' she said in her plump black country accent.

'Ah! I'm only an emeritus professor you know, not a proper one, not any more, not since I retired. Not since two thousand and … two thousand and … er … Hmm. Well a long time actually.' He blushed at his own volubility.

'I don't know about that, Professor. If the Queen abdicates, she's still a Queen isn't she. Now mind that cup, it's hot, don't go spilling it.'

Am I a child, he thought, perplexed rather than irritated, to be talked to like that, condescended to? Then he thought, when *did* I retire? Ten years ago, or twelve? Or less. I can't remember. I must be … how old? Am I seventy-seven, or seventy-five perhaps, or eighty-three? Somebody must have a notion, it'll be written down.

This was maddening, this erosion of memories, the way they were gnawed by time into weird shapes, like sandstone.

The orderly moved away, and Bad Bob watched her with narrowed eyes.

'She's all right that one.' He sucked at his dentures. 'Nice bum.'

'Hmm,' said Winegarden, thinking for a moment of the shapely cello that was Miriam's bottom. In her younger days. More recently, of course, it had withered and sunk. But lovely still, lovely to him. And gone now.

'I don't know why we're here,' he said.

''Cause we were losing it, pal, that's why we're here.'

Winegarden took a sip of tea.

'Sit down a moment, Bob.'

Bad Bob eased his thin body into the next chair.

Winegarden said, 'I don't mean why we *are* here, I mean, why we remain here. We're men, Bob, men. Not *kinder* in a *garten*.' He twisted round uncomfortably, his neck resisting, to face Bob.

'Look,' he said, 'we could … leave.'

'Leave? What're you talking about, Prof?'

'I want to leave, I have *business* to attend to.'

'You wouldn't make it to the lobby. The orderlies, the security door, that keypad thing … Anyhow, what bloody business?'

'Business,' said Winegarden stubbornly. Her grave, he thought, that was the least he could do, visit her grave, pay his respects. Explain things to her, so that she knew. If he didn't, it would be too late; Bob was right, they'd only get out of here feet first.

'Course they'd bloody stop you. Escape from bloomin' Colditz? You're on your own, Steve Flippin' McQueen.'

Winegarden looked at Bob for a few moments, watched him shake his puzzled head.

'Fair enough. But, Bob, will you help me?'

Bob hauled himself back out of his chair – was that a tear of emotion in his eye? – and grasped Winegarden's burly shoulder. 'Help you? Course I'll bloody help you, you nutty old professor. Isn't anyone in this place with a better theoretical knowledge of escapology than Bad Bob Cohen.'

Which was precisely why Winegarden had chosen to broach the subject with this gnarled stick of a man, for all his over-familiarity and lack of a sense of personal space. Bad Bob tapped his nose and muttered, 'Zombies, eh!' Going vacant-eyed and slack-lipped, he shuffled off with a lop-sided gait, his arms held floppily in front of him, lolling and jerking between the rows of chairs where impassive inmates sat immersed in their private universes. The orderly shook her sweet head indulgently. 'Bob, Bob,' she said with gentle reproof. But Bad Bob was too busy with sightless eyes bumping into furniture.

Winegarden watched him with abstracted bemusement. Escape, he thought. It would need to be soon. You had to choose your moment. You missed it, and there'd not be another. He thought about his forebear, Heinz-Josef, he of the complaining wife, escaping the Nazis, fleeing across Europe, by train, on the knife-edge between being caught and not being caught.

This place was different, obviously. They weren't Nazis, or if they were, it was the genteel sort. Caring Nazis. Benign sadists who inflicted on you tepid tea too weak to drink. Nazis who talked down to you and infantilised you, and you couldn't resist because you were indeed becoming like a child, again. If he waited longer, he would have lost the power to act.

After the escape, he thought, he'd go home, to St Augustine's Road. The police would be waiting, of course, he'd observe from a distance, from behind a hedge. There would be lights on in the house. There would be Miriam, his wife, sitting on a sofa, peering through her spectacles. No, no, no, no. How could this be, Miriam was dead, it was so confusing. Ach, there were holes in his brain where brain used to be.

***

The professor was stretched out on his bed, one arm behind his neck. He'd dreamt yet again of escape. Repetitive dreams, exhilarating yet full of foreboding. In them he was always looking for ways out. Alleys, stairways, garden gates. Over walls, in front doors, out via kitchens. Across lawns, through hedges, into fields, up steep hills. Lungs bursting, dogs barking. Zombies, Nazis, orderlies closing.

Now he lay alert, thinking it through. Security seemed quite lax for this class of institution. Perhaps he was seen as low risk, despite the gravity of his act. Low risk because killing one's wife was not a crime likely to be commonly repeated. So: this place was a kind of open prison, with only a security door and a keypad ...

He was now distracted by an insistent question: why had he killed Miriam? If only he could remember, but it was difficult, like peering through a fog. The bright beam of his intellect was useless here, it just scattered light and nothing clear emerged. He stared at his hands, palms up, his once-innocent, gentle hands, as if they contained the secret. It's the plaques on the brain, thought Winegarden. Beta-amyloid. Like blue plaques. Marking all the spots, the spots where famous thoughts used to reside. And memory. Now memories were more like traces, echoes. Subtle signs that there was something there to remember – the paths of subatomic particles caught on the recorders of the Large Hadron Collider, never the elusive particles themselves. Ectoplasm. Slug trails on the patio beneath Miriam's rose bushes … Sometimes not even that: marks that washed away leaving nothing behind, no trace even in your own soul, like messages you scratched on sand with a stick, with the tide coming in.

The idea *three ladies* came into his mind and he snatched at it, perhaps it held the key? Torn Curtain, was that it? The name of the poet. Irish poet, Torn Curtain? Something Curtain? Anyway. Ah yes! Who wrote of three ladies, of an age, their marbles scattered to all corners, in golden dressing gowns like angel wings flowing out behind them. No, no, no, no, no. No. No, no. It couldn't be Curtain, that wasn't a name, even a poet's name. He felt angry tears behind his lids and beat them back as a knock came at his bedroom door.

'Yes?'

Bad Bob poked his head into the room.

'Evening, Prof. May I?'

'Good evening, yes come in Bob, please.' Winegarden pulled himself into a sitting position and swung his legs over the side of the bed. He reached quickly for his spectacles on the bedside cabinet. Bob sat down in the armchair.

'How would you go about it, Prof? What's the grand plan?'

'Escaping? Hmm, I don't know. By being there and not there, I suppose.'

'There and not there, there and not there,' repeated Bad Bob as if he'd been asked a riddle. 'Look, don't know what you're on about half the time, Prof, but there's an armful of options. Harry Houdini, dislocate your thumb, off come the handcuffs. Or the Count of Monte Cristo. Take a potion. They think you're dead. Put you in a sack, chuck you in the sea. Wake up, cut yourself out. Easy peasy ...'

Lemon squeezy, thought Winegarden glumly to himself, but this fortress was not actually on the sea.

'Or,' continued Bad Bob, 'the wooden horse of Stalag Luft III. Or the Shawshank Redemption. Escape from Colditz, Escape from Alcatraz ... That feller that escaped from a French jail in a helicopter flown by his wife, taught herself to fly specially. What a wife will do for a husband, eh. Or take Alfie Hinds ...'

Winegarden looked away. He would never be rescued by his wife – whose fragile neck bones he'd crushed in his old man's grip – nor would he escape over the water, or through the air flying, or under the earth digging, or through shit, swimming. Or by playing dead.

'Alfie Hinds,' Bad Bob was saying, 'famous robber, did Heal's furniture store on the Tottenham Court Road. Could do this thing with his mandible, kind of dislocate it. Gave him a sort of horse-face. Like this.' Bad Bob pulled down his lower jaw and tensed his chin. 'Like another feller altogether. Only problem being that he was blind as a flipping bat without his glasses, like that forger bloke in the Great Escape ...'

Winegarden took a deep resigned breath. Bob had the autodidact's crammed scrapyard of a mind. This could take some time.

But Bad Bob stopped in mid-flow and stroked his chin. 'Let's see, let's see, what about *bolsters*? Two or three pillows, fit your pyjamas round 'em, cushion for a head, or a blown-up party balloon, plenty of them around this place, Lord knows why they bother, rolled up towels for arms ...'

Bolsters in the bed, palimpsests of ourselves, thought Winegarden. Then, lobsters. Lobsters?

'What you reckon?' asked Bad Bob.

Ah, anagram of bolsters. They were troubling Winegarden more and more, these involuntary mental rearrangements. Gravestones so *get ravens*. Non-empirical *minor pelican*. Even cats became acts. Lobsters. He gave a twitch of delicious revulsion at the thought of this most non-kosher of all the non-kosher crustaceans. The scarlet woman, resplendent on the plate, tempting you. Crack me open, eat my soft white flesh. Oh God! Like a shiksa. The idea was full of taint, pollution. It was somehow fitting that his escape should involve a lobster in the bed. Jacob Winegarden: *no crab in aged Jew*.

'Yes,' he said, 'we'll leave lobsters in the bed, that'll throw them off the scent.'

'Ha! Lobsters, that'd be good!' cackled Bob.

After Bob had left, Winegarden lay down again. Hmm, he found himself thinking, if you were to wrap a cat – with buttered toast strapped to its back – in copper wire, you would, on dropping it from a high window, have a kind of feline dynamo. Unable to land either way up, it would hover a little above the ground, revolving rapidly first one way then the other, generating an alternating current in perpetuity, or at least until the animal, done in by hunger and fatigue, fell stiffly to the ground. Buttered side down, little legs sticking up towards the sky. Winegarden sighed: even his thought experiments were becoming denatured, zombified.

He drifted into sleep, dreaming of hands, and necks, and a sombre granite tombstone engraved in Hebrew and English with the legend 'in the name of the soul of Miryam Ester bat Alexandr'. He woke with a start. The Hebrew letters: *tav, nun, tzade, kuf, yod, hei*: may her soul be bound in the binding of life. Her dates. Nineteen hundred and something to two thousand and something. He was not so good on dates any more.

In his case, he wondered, would the soul be caught, like a zombie, or like a cat with buttered toast on its back, in an unending unstable equilibrium between life and death? He thought again of the three ladies of the Irish poem, in their gold dressing gowns, escaping from their Dublin nursing home, taking a car and driving west, throwing themselves into the Shannon at the Emerald Star marina in Tarmonbarry, halfway between here and there, east and west.

***

The next day, Bad Bob smuggled pillows, a small cushion and an old lady's wig into Winegarden's bedroom. The plan was advancing. Bob had cracked the keypad code. 'Did my zombie impression,' he explained, 'while one of the staff was leaving. They don't notice you when you do that. It's the four corner buttons, starting top left …'

There was a knock at the door. 'Professor Winegarden?' said a woman's voice. The door opened, and the black orderly entered, dressed in shiny blue fatigues; smiling: a neat deception. 'You have a visitor.' She held her hand out in beckoning welcome and a woman walked in.

It was Miriam.

Ye gods, thought Winegarden, do not make me mad. She came slowly on arthritic hips but she was alive, not dead. Or undead. Oh God. He felt a sharp metaphysical pain: was this his soul leaving him, so casually? Should he say Kaddish, for him, for her? *Yisgadal v'yiskaddash sh'meh rabbah. B'alma d'vra khiruseh …*

Bad Bob winked at him and followed the orderly out of the room, sprightly, lapsing into a zombie wobble near the door.

'Jacob, darling,' murmured Miriam. She took his hand. 'How are you?'

He said nothing for a time. Then he asked her, with despair in his eyes, 'Why am I here?'

'Because you're … unwell. You need looking after.' She rubbed the back of his hand with her thumb, with pressure gentle but firm, as if trying to ease away the liver spots.

'And why are *you* here?' he said.

'To see you of course.'

'No, I mean, *how* are you here.' Resurrected, he thought.

'Margaret kindly gave me a lift, she'll pick me up later, I'll meet her in the car park and she'll take me back to Birmingham.'

'I'm a bit confused.'

'Yes, Jacob darling,' said Miriam. 'You are a little. It's why you're here.'

He examined his fingers and then shifted his gaze to the side of her neck, looking for marks or signs.

'But you're all right? You're quite … well?' he asked.

'Yes, I'm fine, darling, I'm just fine.'

He shook his head. 'I don't understand.'

'What don't you understand?'

'Everything.'

'Darling!' She smiled.

He wondered if he shouldn't propose that they escape this place together, arm-in-arm. Possibly she might trust him again. Oh dear, it was so muddled in his mind.

'Are you comfortable?' she asked. 'Are the other people nice at all? Anyone you get along with? That chap who was here, looks a bit daft, but nice enough …'

Winegarden stared towards the window. It was still light, there was blue in the sky. This night would be the time, the moment. He lay back on the bed. *Durcan!* he thought, that was it! That was the name of the poet. Yes, Durcan, not Curtain! Yes, Paul Durcan!

That was a small victory at any rate over the inrushing tide.

A Golem Running on Custard

If Miriam had asked Winegarden about the cottage, he would have evaded her gaze and mumbled that it was, um, small and, um, a bit damp. And, ahem, perfectly OK. He would not have been able to tell his wife the colour of its front door: bright red against the whitewashed stone walls, and facing away from the North Atlantic gales that blew in across the hills of the tiny Hebridean island. He would have registered, though, the chill draughts, and the way he had to stoop beneath the low ceilings as he padded back and forth, thickset and bearish.

It was a cold March, Easter was early, and Winegarden had come to this place for a working break with Sergio Onetti, his friend and colleague at the School of Theoretical Physics. Sergio was the younger man, taut and nervy, quick-moving, knuckle-cracking, with black eyes that burned brightly when an idea seized him.

Now he had one.

The two men had been scribbling in notebooks in the living room, watching Sergio's little daughter, six-year-old Anna, through the open door to the kitchen. She was playing at the breakfast table with a mixing bowl and a bag of flour and a jug of water. She was a lovely child, helpful and inquisitive, and she asked the men, in quite a grown-up way, what they were working on. When they answered that they were doing pencil-and-paper experiments – like her cooking, but without the mixing bowl and the rest – she cocked her head, heavy with its weight of black curls, and said, 'Oh, I see.' She laughed and screwed up her black eyes that were so like her father's, and poked her tongue out between her teeth in concentration. Her face daubed with flour and water, she seemed the only one of them not to feel the cold and damp, humming to herself in a thin frock: the two men wore layers of jumpers and woollen scarves knotted close round their necks. Her father called out more than once to her to put more clothes on, but she replied, 'I'm too hot in here, I'm boiling.'

Sergio had stopped his jottings and was looking up abstractedly, seeing Anna and not seeing her. He exclaimed a single word in his Scots-Italian accent: 'Custard!'

Winegarden lifted his eyes from the scribbles of formulae and diagrams, and glanced at Onetti. The two men nodded, and exchanged the briefest of smiles. Their communication had been distilled over the years to this cryptic semaphore, with its own shells of meaning.

Onetti poured himself a glass of whisky, and held it up to the fading light to the west. He took a sip.

Winegarden said, 'Mmm, custard, yes, that might do it.'

It was custard that led Winegarden, with Onetti's help, and the unwitting prompting of Anna, to rethink the problem of the Golem. Winegarden was already well known for his explorations of cats and zombies, doing pioneering work at the unmapped boundary between quantum mechanics and metaphysics; but this was a greater theoretical challenge. The problem can be simply stated. The traditional recipe for the Golem's creation is to take mud and soil, form it into the rough shape of a hefty man, and say aloud letters of the Hebrew alphabet – for example, מ-ל-ג – *gimel, lamed, mem* – G'l'm. Following Rabbi Loew of Prague, incantations are then murmured using the *shemhamforash*, the Kabbalistic 72-letter name for God, and this contains within it names of angels, and of forms of the soul. The Golem is then buried before being animated, and the letters *aleph, mem, sav*, forming the word *emes*, truth, are marked on the creature's forehead. When the Golem is decommissioned, so to speak, the *aleph* is rubbed away, leaving *mes*: death.

The agnostic Winegarden did not have much faith in the power of rabbinical incantations, though it was just possible that they changed probabilities and caused anomalous quantum effects in the world of large-scale objects. But, in essence, the raw materials did not have the chemical properties to cohere in the shape of a man, even a mud man, nor the elasticity to bear movement.

However, if you were to mix, say, cornflour and water with the mud, you would have a muddy custard that was both elastic and resilient. By applying forces, you would cause it to thicken and solidify. You could use it to make a Golem that would move freely and sinuously without falling apart. It would be impregnable to sudden assault, a sort of Jewish Kevlar, resisting the penetration of bullets and knives: the harder they thrust at him, the harder his mud-custard thorax would repel them. Briefly, Winegarden wondered whether semen might be the ideal non-Newtonian fluid for animating a Golem, but decided that the practical difficulties would be considerable.

More profound was the question of the Golem's soul. A Golem is widely seen as a base being, driven by instinct and without intellect and self-awareness. Living, but not autonomous of thought and action. More a zombie, though a zombie built from scratch rather than resurrected from once-living tissue. Would it be possible to infuse it with *pneuma*, the breath of life, or would it always be no more than a living robot?

Sergio and Winegarden sat in deep concentration, scribbling notes on scraps of paper. When they ran out of ideas, Sergio looked up, his eyes creasing into a mischievous twinkle and a dimple showing in his cheek: signs that Winegarden knew well. 'Jacob, Jacob, what if ...' asked Onetti, '... what if we set a Golem to *run on a tank of custard*?'

'Aha,' said Winegarden. He pursed his lips and nodded. The Golem with its clattering, flat-footed gait would surely cause the custard to stiffen instantly. 'Now,' added Winegarden, lifting his chin towards the ceiling, 'supposing the Golem were to run over the custard on tiptoes. Or like a ballet dancer, with mincing, dainty little steps?'

Sergio shrieked with laughter. 'A camp Golem!'

Winegarden was puzzled for a second: 'camp' meant one thing in his mind, and it was to do with Alsatian dogs, thudding boots and barbed wire, rather than ballerinas.

'What's so funny, Daddy?' scolded Anna from the kitchen. 'I don't get the joke.' This made Sergio laugh harder, and now Winegarden joined in, teary-eyed, his chest shaking in contained mirth.

'Please will you just stop that, Daddy, you're being very silly,' said Anna, running in covered in cornflour paste, and shaking her head in a world-weary way. Sergio ruffled her curly hair and bent over to kiss her cheek, and then she was gone again.

The manner in which the Golem ran, the two men concluded, would affect subatomic particles in their orbits, causing electrons to lose energy and fall back tighter around the nucleus of the atoms, like wagons circling on the prairies, like cornered Jews at a pogrom. They agreed the impact on the custard would vary with the gait and size of the running creature. A Golem is one thing, a cat, with its light pattering run, quite another. It would cause improbable quantum effects, such as the flinging out from the fluid of little plumes of matter, and these might well take the shape of mini-beings; mini-monsters, or mini-Golems. Now if these could be scaled up …

And so they went on, speculating till the sky grew dark, satisfied that they at least had a title for their academic paper: 'A Golem Running on Custard'. They liked the notion that, in years to come, some bright young scientist, seeing only the title, might misinterpret the paper as being about novel forms of fuel (as in Golems running on biomass, or cooking oil) and end up making a substantial if accidental contribution to climate science.

Pleased with themselves, they got up and went to the kitchen and pretended to be commis-chefs while Anna ordered them around, and the supper of eggs and beans somehow got made. After they'd eaten, and Anna had been bathed and cleansed of cornflour paste and tucked into bed, the two friends sat listening to the howl of the wind and drinking a glass of malt whisky. As was their custom at such moments, they let their minds roam free, coming up with extravagant experiments that would never be funded, involving for example gamma rays, rapid eye movements, and zombies in dark glasses moving at the speed of light through a vacuum.

At bedtime, Sergio went out into the night for a cigarette, and arctic air blew through the cottage, slamming shut the front door. Anna cried out in her sleep, 'Daddy, Daddy!' The entrance porch was wet with whipped rain, and Sergio returned, soaked through. 'It's a foul night,' he said from the foot of the stairs as he went to check on his daughter. 'It was supposed to be springtime, even up here.'

Winegarden thought about his wife and wondered what she was doing at that moment, somewhere in London, or Birmingham, out with her sister, or a friend, at the theatre or a restaurant. He felt a quiver of anxiety at the thought that someone else was privy to her activities when he was not. They were not often apart, though even when they were together, he found her still enigmatic, still unfathomable.

The next day, the two men worked steadily, refining their ideas, ruminating silently until one would speak and the other would nod briefly, and there was much scribbling and crossing out, and once or twice they tapped at scientific calculators. Often they found themselves in dead ends from which they retreated in order to advance down new avenues. The rain came in ferocious gusts, and the windows rattled in their frames. Anna was not as perky or chatty as usual, she didn't sing to herself or play at baking. She brought the men glasses of orange juice, but she was solemn-faced and pale. In the afternoon she went and curled up on the sofa, wrapped in Sergio's big coat, watching them.

They all retired early, dispirited by the weather. They had the sense of being under siege. In the night, Winegarden heard the little girl's voice, 'Daddy, Daddy!', and Sergio's steps on the creaking floorboards of the bedroom. In the morning, she was burning to the touch and lay shivering under a pile of blankets. The men forgot about the Golem and nursed her.

'You should call the doctor,' said Winegarden.

'I've tried,' said Onetti. His eyes were dull with fatigue and worry. 'There's no dialling tone, the lines are never good here.'

They looked at each other, uncertain what to do.

'In any case, the doctor's on Skye, we'd have to get the ferry and ...' Sergio trailed off, sweeping his arm towards the grey rain-lashed panes. There would be no ferries while this weather lasted. They sat with Anna in turns in the bedroom, under the sloping ceiling. She responded a little to an aspirin that Sergio had crushed for her. But she was burning up.

Winegarden tried to read at the living-room table in the fading light. Later, he trod up the stairs and found Sergio stretched out asleep on the bed alongside his daughter. She was twisting this way and that and murmuring syllables that had no meaning. Winegarden sat down in the armchair and watched over them, listening to the wind, fearful.

In the middle of the night Anna threw off the blankets and sat up rigid. Her hair was stuck to her forehead. She stared at nothingness. Sergio woke, confused and groggy with sleep. He got up and fetched some water for her, while she uttered low fretful moans that sounded more animal than human. She began to tremble violently and lay back down in the bed, curled into a ball, still quivering with fever. Her father covered her with the blankets. He went downstairs, Winegarden with him, and tried the telephone again. He stood listening, arm tensed against his side. Shaking his head, he put down the receiver and looked at his friend with red-rimmed helplessness.

'I could drive to the next cottage ...' said Winegarden.

'And what could they do?' replied Sergio.

'I don't know, I don't know.'

Jacob reached out to grip his friend's arm.

'She's all I have,' Sergio murmured.

Jacob moved towards the door. 'I'm going for help.'

'Where?'

'I don't know.'

Winegarden went outside with the keys to Sergio's car. He bent against the gale, the rain stinging his eyes. A nervous driver and out of practice, he crawled along in second gear, reaching out to wipe the misting screen with his hand. The car seemed like a dangerous machine, tugging him forward along the dark curves of the road. He saw a lighted window in a cottage and turned into the driveway and over the cattle grid. A dog barked as he approached. He rang the doorbell. Its two-tone chime sounded cruelly ordinary. He thought, whenever I hear that chime again somewhere, I'll think of poor Anna lying sick. The dog barked louder but no one came. Winegarden was soaked through. A mile down the road, another house. A grey-haired woman in a dressing gown opened the door to him and the wind rushed into her hallway like a gang of intruders.

'Do you know what time it is?' she asked. Her face was lined like that of a smoker's.

It was two in the morning. Winegarden stammered his apologies. 'My friend, his little girl, she's very sick. I think she might be …'

'Nonsense. Has she a fever?'

'A fever, yes, a very high one.'

'Cool compresses. Head, neck, hands.'

She moved to the sideboard and took a packet of tablets out of a drawer.

'You have some of these?'

'I think so.'

She thrust them into his hand.

'Now off you go, I have an interesting dream to return to.'

By the time he'd thanked her, and mumbled more apologies, the door had been shut and he was back in the howling darkness of the night.

He got to the cottage and took a bowl of water upstairs and sat with Sergio, mopping Anna's brow and her neck and hands. She was still thrashing around, arcing her back, and her black eyes were glowing like wet pebbles. Winegarden gave her one of the tablets and pressed the towel to her again and again until gradually her skin felt less burning hot and she became calmer. At length she gave out a deep sigh and lay still under the blankets. Her father lifted the sheet to check on her, and tucked it back around her shoulders. He sat on the edge of the bed, his arms crossed, rocking backwards and forwards.

Winegarden was awoken at dawn by sunlight filtering in through the dormer window. Anna seemed better now, the crisis had passed, the film of sweat on her forehead was gone. Sergio was still sitting on the bed, gently stroking her hair. His face was drawn. He got up and went over to the window and looked out at the grey sky.

'You slept a little?' asked Jacob.

Sergio shrugged. 'Sleep? I don't know.'

Then: 'Daddy, I'm thirsty.'

Startled, the two men stared at Anna. She opened her eyes and they were bright but not burning with fever.

'I'm really, really thirsty.'

'Yes, darling, I'll get you some water!' shouted Sergio, and he came over to her and hugged her tight.

'No need to suffocate me,' she said in her grown-up manner, and the two men laughed; it was laughter filled with relief. Sergio brought Anna her water, and she gulped it down. Within moments she was fast asleep again. Her father laid his hand on her shoulder. He seemed on the point of tears. 'I think she's going to … going to be all right,' he said.

Winegarden nodded, his throat too tight to speak. They sat in silence for a long time. Sergio smiled to himself and glanced at his friend. His eyes shone. He said, "*Considerate la vostra semenza: fatti non foste a viver come bruti, ma per seguir virtute e canoscenza.*" Dante. I don't know why it comes to my mind. "Consider where you come from: you were not born to live like brutes, but to follow virtue and knowledge."'

Jacob said, 'Are you thinking of the Golem?'

'"Live like brutes"? Perhaps,' said Sergio, 'perhaps.' At that moment it seemed to Winegarden that the two men were like brothers.

Sergio went on, 'My family were Jews in Modena, my ancestors reached there from Spain, five hundred years ago. There's a dreadful thing about my family, I never told you this, Jacob: my great-uncle, Alessandro, marched with Mussolini.' He shook his head. 'Yes, Jews took part in the March on Rome. Two hundred of them. It beggars belief. They thought he would protect them from their enemies.'

'Like a Golem,' said Winegarden softly.

'Jews for Mussolini!' continued Sergio. 'That's why I'm here, and not there. My family survived the war, but straight afterwards, my father left Italy, came to Scotland, to Edinburgh. Out of disgust, out of a sense of shame. And so I am Scottish-Jewish-Italian. Bravo, bravo.'

He looked taken aback by how much he'd revealed.

'We all carry our ancestors' shame,' said Winegarden.

'I'm sorry,' Sergio said, 'I didn't mean to ear-bash you with that stuff ...' He trailed off and there was a moment's stillness.

***

Anna improved by the hour and by the afternoon she was downstairs and perky again. While she lay on the sofa, Winegarden and Onetti tried to go back to work, seated at the living-room table. But something was wrong. The carefree brio had gone, things had changed. The next day, with Anna quite recovered, Winegarden felt ill at ease, as if another storm were brewing, an inner storm. The two men seemed at odds, pursuing ideas that were at cross-purposes.

'No, no, Sergio,' Winegarden would mutter irritably. 'It's about using events at the subatomic level to understand the behaviour of large bodies, such as springs or levers. Or cats, or zombies ...'

'Yes, yes. Or Golems. I realise that.' Onetti puffed out his breath and shook his head.

'Or souls.'

'Jacob,' chided Sergio, 'I do not find "the soul" a particularly scientific concept.'

'Oh but in principle it certainly is,' said Winegarden.

And so the bickering continued.

Anna was merry and singing while she played, and getting under their feet. This only added to the strained atmosphere. She brought the men their glasses of orange juice and stood watching them drink it. 'Thank you, Anna, it's good,' said Winegarden, but still she stood there and he wished her gone. She then discovered a small cardboard box of marbles hidden in a drawer, and played with them on the tiled kitchen floor. The knocking of the glass marbles set the professor's teeth on edge.

'Anna!' he called out in a loud but friendly voice.

The jangling continued. Winegarden got up from the table and shut the door to the kitchen. It slammed to with a louder noise than he'd intended. Seconds later the door opened and Anna appeared, with her marbles.

'I want to be with you.'

'OK, darling,' said Sergio, 'as long as you're quiet and let us work.'

'I'm bored,' she said.

'Make a cake?'

'No, I don't feel like it!'

She sat on the floor near them and let the marbles drop one by one from a height. Winegarden put down his pencil and waited for a second. There was another clink of a marble hitting the floor. He said, too fiercely, 'Anna! Please! Not so much noise, you know we're trying to work!'

The little girl looked at him and her big eyes were shiny with tears of reproach. Winegarden frowned, feeling as though he'd crushed a delicate fluttering thing; yet still inexplicably angry. Onetti said nothing, but his look was pained. Their conversation, already stuttering, became sparse and, as it were, clenched. They spoke with their gazes averted. After lunch Winegarden tried to ingratiate himself with Anna, but she wouldn't be won over, sharply turning her head away from him.

The weather had cleared and calmed, and the following day they were to leave the island.

***

The morning of departure was bright and blustery and they drove back to the ferry in near silence. Anna hummed to herself on the back seat. Later, as they crossed the newly opened Skye bridge to the mainland, Winegarden turned and saw that she had fallen asleep, and he said to Onetti, 'Look, Sergio, I'm sorry, I'm not normally snappy like that, I don't know why I …'

'We've been through a lot,' said Sergio. 'A lot of strain. Intellectual. Emotional. Let's turn the page.'

The tension between them eased, but still Winegarden felt out of sorts, disrupted within. Sergio dropped him off in Edgbaston at midnight. He went upstairs and lay on the bed, and fell into a worried half-sleep. It was still dark when he awoke. And a terrible image was in his mind.

Of Miriam, many years before. Each breast painfully engorged with useless milk curdling in its duct.

Then he remembered that which he tried to push to the deep parts of his mind. The callous normality of the synagogue elders. It's not thirty days, they said. He did not understand. They explained it to him. As it says in the *Mishneh Torah,* we do not mourn *nefalim,* foetuses. Until a child is thirty days old, it is not fully in the world, it does not have a soul, and therefore it does not have a funeral if it dies. In the old days, the grave would not even be marked, the parents not knowing where their dead baby lay.

Miriam's child was stillborn. Born still. Dead, but without ever having had a soul. Buried perfunctorily, with no funeral.

The wives of the synagogue elders took Miriam aside. One said, cabbage leaves in the bra, that'll help dry the milk. Another said, try ice, that usually works for the discomfort. And a third, avoid stimulation, it makes it worse. She withered them all with her scornful look. Her engorged breasts were like a badge of mourning for her. But she did not want to name him.

'Why on earth?' she asked Jacob harshly. 'To help us find our child in the world to come?'

'Perhaps it will help us ... deal with grief,' he said.

'No!' she cried, 'it will not!'

Winegarden insisted, it was one of those rare moments when he felt he had to take a tiny particle of control over events, to be more than their passive victim. He said, 'I want our baby to have a name.'

'Fine. Do it,' she said. 'You do it.' She turned away.

He named it Joshua.

How can you breathe life into dead clay? That was Winegarden's question, his quest, from the moment he saw that pale corpse, touched the marble coldness of its skin, wept his first bitter tears on behalf of this poor uncircumcised being.

For Miriam, it was something not to be spoken about. There was no language for it. Instead, she tended her roses and grew enigmatic, always just out of his reach somehow.

For Winegarden, there came thought experiments. Starting with *what if, what if he'd lived.* He would have been known as Josh, perhaps. What would he have become, what would he be doing now? Would Winegarden have nursed him through childhood illnesses? Would he have watched the boy burn up with fever and then, with relief, seen the storm pass and the child smile at him again? Or perhaps succumb, leaving unquantifiable grief? The awareness of Joshua was constant, a nagging presence, but faint, every minute of every day. The death was a failure of thought on Winegarden's part, a failure of imagination: he was guilt-stricken by his inability to work out a way to animate this … this lump of disanimated clay.

It was some small consolation to Jacob that in time, much time, atoms that were once part of Joshua would be freed from their retaining bonds and float up to travel the cosmos. And one day towards the end of time, just before the heat death of the universe, Joshua's atoms would meet atoms of Miriam's and of Winegarden's and be reunited in new bonds. He tried once to explain this to Miriam, this soothing conceit, but she would have none of it, grew angry, and spat sarcastic words at him. 'What are you trying to tell me, Jacob, that our son is a wandering Jew? Condemned by his sins to unquietly travel the universe?' Winegarden remembered his biblical studies, Hosea's bleak prophecies. 'My God will cast them off, because they have not hearkened to him; they shall be wanderers among the nations.'

'No,' cried Miriam, 'No, Jacob! What kind of consolation is that?'

For weeks afterwards, they had not made love. One day, it happened, more out of anger than desire, unsettling, not loving. He said, 'Are you all right? Did you …? Was it …?'

'No,' she said, meaning to wound. 'No, you didn't satisfy me, I didn't come.' And as if withdrawing the knife would undo the hurt, she said, 'But no doubt you will again, at some point,' and she turned her back on him.

The pain corroded him: the pain of loving her as madly as he had ever done, and of hating her for her callousness. For her withdrawal. For not having borne him a live son.

He buried himself in his experiments. Perhaps cats would hold the key, or zombies, or Golems. Perhaps, perhaps.

***

Winegarden sat up in the bed, propping his head against the pillow, sombre, feeling shame at his outburst at the cottage on the Scottish island. He wanted badly to explain things to Sergio but feared that things could not be explained. He sighed, and started doing anagrams in his head to still his brain. After a while he lay down again. He felt a fragile calm. He was doing the best he knew, he'd come a long way with Golems, with understanding how to imbue them with the breath of life, with a soul. His paper with Onetti would light the way for others. In a distant future, perhaps his grief would have some purpose. Perhaps, perhaps.

Miriam would be back in the morning. He was looking forward to seeing her, to hearing her sweet ironical voice, to feeling her eyes fix unknowably on him; to the illusion that he was meaningful in her pale grey universe.

'Say kaddish for me,' Harry had rasped on his deathbed. 'I know my son the professor doesn't believe in all that rigmarole, but please, Jacob, on Rosh Hashanah, go to shul, say kaddish for me.'

Winegarden had not stepped inside a synagogue for years. The prospect intrigued but also perturbed him. Rosh Hashanah, the Jewish new year, was a festival of remembrance. Your past acts to be recalled and weighed in the balance, your fate decided. Will you be inscribed in the book of life? Or in the book of death?

It had been a tough time for Winegarden.

He would wake in the night, relive the death of his yet-to-be-born child: the concerned expressions of the midwives, the faltering, urgent lights of the monitors, the calling of the duty registrar. The interminable, hushed wait. The sense of being in a tight binding of dread. And later, the accusing, disappointed faces of the relatives. The sense of failure, culpability, shame. He hated the pitying looks especially, because they meant he was now a member of the underclass of the pitied. Miriam was haughty with the professional commiseraters, their touch on the forearm, their mournful gaze.

'They are trying to do the right thing, I suppose,' said Winegarden.

'They have no clue.'

She withdrew. Their exchanges became sparse and clipped. It had been three years of armed truce, a couple more of tense coexistence. Each set up camp at night on their own side of the matrimonial bed, turned away from the other, the invisible central borderline uncrossable. Jacob recalled the writings of the rabbis: 'When our love was strong, we could lie comfortably on the edge of a sword. However, now that our love is not as strong, even a bed that is sixty cubits long is not big enough!'

'It's Rosh Hashanah on Wednesday,' he said to Miriam.

'Even I know that.'

'I'm going to synagogue to say kaddish, it was the last thing I promised my father.'

'Fair enough.' She stared out of the window. Pallid autumn sunlight filtered through the branches of the sycamores.

'Jacob,' she said, still not looking at him, 'would you drop in at the Jewish deli on the Pershore Road.'

'I would, of course.'

'It is yomtov after all,' she said, smiling to herself, as if conscious of the lameness of the pretext. She had never been one for high holy days, or any sort of holy days.

'Haven't been to Gee's for ages.' He felt a pricking of emotion, mysterious and obscure, like a recollection struggling to be born.

***

It was a brisk forty minutes on foot to the deli. As Winegarden walked with his busy, burly stride along the Hagley Road, he no longer saw the cheap hotels, the orthodontist practices, the low-rise flats, the blurry stream of traffic. Memories, he thought, often had that elusive quality, more a faint odour or a delicate staining of the present with the past. Hmm. What was the act of recollection if not a form of quantum entanglement of states of perception across space-time? Memories changed according to the point at which you tried to apprehend them. The grasping of a memory at one moment made it less defined at another, like squeezing a long balloon at one end, causing it to bulge elsewhere. This gave rise to tantalising practical possibilities: the implantation of new memories in those whose minds have been damaged by trauma or dementia, the erasure of painful memories, or their detoxification. Perhaps, as the rabbis implied in their treatises on Rosh Hashanah as the festival of remembering, the sounding of the ceremonial ram's horn, the shofar, is a mechanism for unlocking quantum effects of memory – the liturgical equivalent of a laser or an electron microscope. Perhaps it could be harnessed therapeutically ...

'Sir, can I help you? Sir?'

Winegarden looked around, surprised to find himself in the queue at Gee's kosher delicatessen. He had the impression that the man behind the counter had asked this question once already, or perhaps more than once.

It was partly his embarrassment that caused him to buy far more than he'd intended. But also, the smell of the shop had taken him back to his childhood. He got home an hour later with schmaltz herring, salt beef, smoked salmon, cream cheese, *heimische* cucumbers, boiled gefilte fish (and horseradish and beetroot condiment to go with it), *chollah* bread with poppy seeds ...

Miriam inspected his purchases. 'Schmaltz herring? Makes your breath smell.'

'There is mouthwash,' Winegarden replied, and blushed. He was not sure why.

'Yes, well, you've got enough to feed an army.'

She helped him unload the produce and put it away. 'I fancy a walk,' she said. 'I suppose you're exhausted from your expedition to Gee's and back.'

'Oh,' said Winegarden. 'No, not at all. Why, would you want company, or ...?'

'That would be nice.'

He peered at her face, but there was no irony lurking beneath her smile.

They strolled side by side, close but not touching, along Saint Augustine's Road, round by the church, up Norfolk Road and through the trees to Edgbaston Reservoir. A path ran round the lake. They stopped and sat on a bench. Quite near to them, a heron stood on one leg, utterly still, like a statue of a heron.

'It's almost professorial, wouldn't you say,' Miriam said.

'Do I look like that?' asked Winegarden.

'Well perhaps not. For a start, you don't keep still. When you're thinking, your foot is always tapping up and down, and you chew your lower lip, and smooth down your eyebrows with your fingertips. You do have that focus, though.'

'A focus on fish?'

'On your experimental thoughts, I expect. Though possibly on gefilte fish.'

'Hmm.'

The heron took off and flew, heavy and laden, like an airfreighter, over the water and away. They watched it go. Miriam bent down, picked a pebble off the path and tossed it into the lake.

'You're casting off your sins?'

'Or throwing the first stone ...' she said.

Jacob also found a pebble, a flat one, and he crouched to skim it low across the surface. It bounced several times.

'My sins are light, obviously.'

Tashlikh, thought Winegarden: the casting of pebbles into the river or the sea, or the reservoir, to expiate sins, the sloughing off of guilt in preparation for the day of judgement.

'Will you come with me?' he asked. 'To the synagogue, I mean.'

'I don't do synagogue. Not interested in God.'

'It's not about religion or God, or believing. I know you don't much care for God and all that. Neither do I, other than philosophically. It's about remembering, about connecting.'

'Mmm.'

He peered at her. 'Is that a yes, Miriam darling?'

***

Winegarden had wanted to go to the Liberal synagogue so that he and Miriam could sit together, but she insisted they

72

went to the old Singer's Hill Orthodox shul on Ellis Street. 'Then I can look down on you men from the balcony. You're like a load of old women, nattering away,' she said. 'Very entertaining.'

'I thought you already looked down on me.'

She frowned. He thought she would close herself off again, back away. He said, 'It was a joke.'

But she smiled, warm and mischievous, and said, 'Jacob, darling, I know it was a joke!' and stroked the side of his face with her hand.

He felt something long unfamiliar: a sudden rearing up of lust.

***

They have returned from the synagogue, and eaten their delicacies. She has stroked his arm and looked at him, her eyes sleepy with desire, and now she is lying on their bed. She is sensuous and sleek, aloof and elusive, playful. For years she has been the subject of Jacob's fevered, impure thought experiments. And for the last hour he's become an empiricist, putting thought into practice. She has been pliant, and compliant, inciting him. She rubs his stomach. 'Hmm,' she says, like a doctor examining a symptom. 'Are you being very pious on this high holy day of obligations, Professor Winegarden?'

There are flavours of schmaltz herring, like the salty old days, tinged with the tang of peppermint mouthwash. They've begun to kiss again.

'I've been dreaming of this,' he says. 'Every day. Every day since … "Oh that you would kiss me with the kisses of your mouth!"'

'Is that Joni Mitchell or someone?'

'The Song of Solomon.'

'What other kind of kisses could there be than the kisses of your mouth?'

'Hmm.'

73

He examines her face, which is turned from him. 'It has been such a long time. Why didn't we … do this earlier?'

'I don't know. The time has to be right.'

'And now it is?'

'Apparently.' She kisses him, very gently, just a brushing of the lips, at the corner of his mouth.

He thinks, love that has grown weak can also grow strong again, why not?

Miriam stretches. 'Conduct some thought experiments on me.'

Somehow, she has been jolted back to him, back into the flow of space-time, out of her alternative, untouchable parallel universe. In her late thirties she is still glorious.

***

Earlier, in the synagogue, he'd put on his driving glasses so that he would be able to spot her on the balcony, across the cubits of airy space. He looked up and saw her, standing at the rail in her pearl grey suit, the red lipstick bright on her pale face. He was reminded of one Yom Kippur service a quarter of century earlier, in this same place. Weak from fasting, he'd felt as despondent as a fifteen-year-old can be because she had not come to her usual central position, and would certainly not come now, and he knew he'd have to wait four whole days, until Shabbes, to see her again.

Miriam spotted Winegarden in the pews below and gave a little wave. Her eyes were on him, as troubling and luscious as in the early days, and enriched with the sediments of memory. An elderly congregant in a fancy prayer shawl and homburg, standing over his neighbour to gossip, looked round at Winegarden for a moment with disapproval, sensing the charge in the couple's gaze.

Winegarden was lulled by the drone of prayer and the low murmur of conversation. This was his creative time, where the thoughts came by themselves. Of cats, and zombies, and quantum memories. Of remembering and not remembering. Of whether cats and zombies could be said to have memories as human beings do. Of what mixture of non-Newtonian fluids might implant memories in the brain of a golem ... But very quickly his mind filled with visions of Miriam, of the demure indecency of her eyes.

A penetrating blast shattered Winegarden's fantasies. He stared at the platform. Two men were standing, facing the congregation, their striped prayer shawls drawn over their heads. One was chanting the names of shofar sounds, with a rising and falling intonation. The other was holding the long curving horn to his lips.

For Winegarden, the trembling, bellowing blasts of the ram's horn were like an admonitory summons, vibrating in his viscera.

Teki-a-a-ah! A single blast.

Teru-a-a-ah! Nine short blasts.

Sh'vor-i-im! Three broken blasts.

Tekiah g'doh-lah! A single sustained blast.

The sounds forced open portals in his mind.

Here, in the past: Joshua, leader of the Israelites, is besieging Jericho, ordering his seven priests to sound their ram's horns in front of the Ark of the Covenant. One long blast: *tekiah g'doh-lah.* And then the people shout, and the walls fall.

Here, in the present: Jacob is holding his son Joshua, cold and dead, and never properly alive.

Winegarden lowered his head and pinched his sore eyes with thumb and forefinger. The mourners' kaddish was recited. The banal words had an incantatory force. As he murmured them, he glanced again at Miriam.

Her head was bowed over her prayer-book. He was startled to see her lips move.

She was saying the prayer. In an undertone, he suspected. But still, saying kaddish. *Yisgadal v'yiskaddash sh'meh rabbah ... .* May his *great name* grow exalted and sanctified. And Jacob could think, not of a God who might or might not exist, but only of the *great name* of his son: Joshua.

***

There was the usual dense press of bodies in the lobby as the men filed through the double doors and the women came downstairs from the balcony. People greeted each other with cries of 'Good yomtov! *Shanah tovah*! Happy new year!' as they headed for the sweet Kiddush wine and pickled cucumbers. Winegarden, fastidious in crowds, found himself trying to shrink from contact. And there was Miriam, being carried towards him on the tide of worshippers, a subversive glint of amusement in her eyes.

'I'm glad I went,' she said, 'if only for the shofar blowing. I feel blasted, but in a beneficial way, like having your ears syringed. Did you see how his cheeks puffed out? I thought his face was going to burst.'

She leaned up to put her hand on his neck and kiss him on the cheek. 'Good yomtov.' He smelt the warm odour of her skin. 'Hope you're prepared for judgement,' she whispered, gripping his hand. 'Is your moral balance sheet in order?' Winegarden felt privileged at her complicity, her sarcasm was a precious gift.

As they walked home, she surprised him, threading her arm through his.

'I'm glad we did that, Jacob darling.'

After a while, he said, 'It's funny, I thought you considered the kaddish was dreadful mumbo jumbo.'

'Well,' she said slowly, 'it's hard to believe that if God exists he really cares for all this sycophantic drivel about how marvellous he is. It might just irritate him.'

'But you said it anyway.'

'Yes, it's the ritual, the sound it makes. It's quite solemn.' She grinned at him. 'Don't worry, I don't *believe*. I'm not suddenly turning *frum* in early middle age, it's just …'

76

'I wouldn't mind if you suddenly turned *frum*. Worse things have happened.' He had a sense of the awkward weight of his words, and fell silent.

***

He led her up the stairs, apprehensive, frightened, conscious of her scars, of his own. For a long time they lay clothed on the bed, not speaking, not knowing how to speak.

Then, unexpectedly, she said, 'It will be five years next week.'

He waited.

'I mean, since ... our son, since ... Joshua died. He would have been five ...'

'Yes,' he said, awed by her courage.

'They tell you grief has to go through stages. But that isn't how it works. Either that, or I'm a kind of freak ...'

This was the first time she had mentioned Joshua's name, the first time she had called him 'our son'.

'Yes, next Wednesday he would have been five,' Winegarden said.

'And starting school ...'

'There is no road map for grief.'

'Darling, that is a plodding turn of phrase, even for a man of science ...' She tried to laugh and the laughter choked. She shook her head, struggling for words.

Jacob felt his eyes prick with tears. He reached out and took her hand, and she did not withdraw it.

So does grief end, thought Jacob, or at least soften?

As if reading his mind, she said, 'I don't mean you're over it. I mean the stuff that incapacitates you, the being struck down – I'm over that, I think. Today at least I'm over that. I can't speak for tomorrow.'

She turned towards him and stroked his face, and kissed his lips. It was as though she had flung open the curtains and let in the light.

***

My beloved put his hand on the latch of the door, and my heart was thrilled within me.

You have grey doves' eyes behind your veil of melancholy. Your garden tastes of samphire and sea anemone.

My beloved smells of rye bread with caraway seeds. His left hand should be under my head, and his right hand should embrace me. My beloved's belly spreads with incipient middle age and his lack of exercise, yet it is pleasing to me. My beloved's eyebrows are like flocks of black sheep in the hills of Judea.

The flesh of your white breast is as sweet as lobster.

My beloved is gone down into my garden, to the beds of spices to feed in the garden and to gather wild flowers.

***

Miriam rested her chin on Jacob's chest and smiled at him. 'You know about the *mitzvah onah*?'

'I vaguely recall something from my Shabbes afternoon Talmud studies with Rabbi Jonathan, but that was twenty-five years ago.'

'*Mitzvah onah* is about a man's duty to provide conjugal rights to his wife.'

'Hmm.'

'Regularly.'

'Hmm.'

'And to satisfy her.'

'And did I?'

'It's amazing what you learn in the ladies' toilets of the orthodox synagogue on a high holy day.'

'And did I, Miriam? I mean were you …?'

'This woman was complaining that her husband had gone off on a business trip for three months, and how could that be reasonable?'

'Indeed …'

'What was she expected to do, she was saying. Take a lover, have an affair? I mean, two *frum* women talking about sex in the synagogue toilets and having a good old giggle about it. The other one said, "I'd divorce mine if he did that." "What, take a lover?" "No, no, I mean go off for three months leaving me high and dry."'

She glanced at him, ironic and affectionate. 'Apparently, it's forbidden for a husband to absent himself for extended periods and thereby deprive his wife of marital relations … Did you know that, Jacob darling?'

'Did you know,' replied Winegarden, 'that it is wrong for a wife to deny her husband intercourse in order to punish or manipulate him?'

'Where does it say that?'

'In the Talmud.'

'You would have made a fine rabbi, Jacob.'

'Hmm.'

'And yes, darling, you did satisfy me. Very much.'

After a moment's silence, Jacob said, 'I suppose I have been rather absent since … for a number of years. There and not there. I'm sorry, my love, it's been hard.'

'Yes, I'm sorry too.' She lay back, her head on her folded arm. 'Today has been a good day though.'

There was a pause.

'I think about him constantly, you know. About Joshua.'

He kissed her on the forehead. 'Thank you,' he said. 'Thank you.'

'I'm so pleased you insisted on naming him.'

Winegarden sighed deeply. It was as though a long-held anxiety had been eased from him. They both wept, and smiled through their tears, and held each other.

Later, Miriam got out of bed, naked. Winegarden felt an uptick of desire. He reached for her hand, wanted to pull her back to him, but she freed herself.

'I'm going to light the yahrzeit candle,' she said.

'For yomtov …'

'For remembrance. For our son. For your father.'

Their love would ebb and flow, he was sure. There would be times when she would grow distant and cold and enigmatic, that was her nature. But then, the moment would come when she would rub up against him, like an animal demanding the warmth of another animal, and he'd respond of course. And for a while he'd feel replete, with a seeding of melancholy, wondering how long the respite would last.

She loved him; then she loved him not. She loved him and, *at the same time*, she loved him not: a mystery of the universe.

Winegarden lay curled on his side in the bed. His bulky body had shrivelled in on itself, the lustre of his dark brown irises was occluded by an adipose rim. His wife, Miriam, was standing beside him, looking down.

'Why hasn't my son been to see me?' he asked.

'Jacob, darling, you have no son, what son?'

'I have a son. Joshua. Yes. He's nearly 50 you know.'

'Darling, Joshua died.'

'Died? When? Why didn't you tell me, Miriam?'

'He died as a baby, Jacob. Hardly even a baby. He was stillborn, remember.'

Winegarden became meek and biddable again, the tetchy tone gone. 'Oh. I see. That's right. Stillborn.'

She smiled tolerantly, her head on one side.

'And my father?' he said.

***

When Winegarden delivered his inaugural professorial lecture, he was disturbed to see his father, Harry, in the audience. Harry sat in the front row, nodding his heavy, white-topped head in encouragement. Winegarden feared another scene, like at their wedding: Miriam had never forgiven the old man for the dredged-up anger of that irruption: *Remember Jerusalem! Dash the children of the harlots of Babylon against the rocks! We are strangers in a strange land!* All that. Harry's wife had just died, he was a little mad with grief and its triggering of the past: the flight from Germany, the distant events raw and present.

So Jacob stood at the lectern, shuffling his notes, conscious as he spoke that he was waiting for something unpleasant to happen. But Harry sat quiet and attentive during the talk, like an assiduous student, jotting comments on a lined pad in a looping hand. The lecture was entitled

'Aardvarks to Zombies (via cats and Golems): Beings of use to non-empirical experimentation'. It ranged widely, covering quantum physics and the soul, quantum locking, and the reversibility of the heat death of the universe. The soul is ever-present and yet is located nowhere in space-time. There is something like a soul in all human beings, it is there by virtue of their being human, it is changed by forces such as suffering which exert quantum effects. The problem of entropy means that systems run down, the heat gradient of the universe flattens; the gradient that drives all processes of the cosmos, including life. Though as the mathematics are probabilistic, there remains the possibility, tiny but finite, that entropy reverses itself in one of the many parallel universes and that life will therefore go on ... Etcetera.

When it was time for questions, Harry raised his arm shyly. 'You say time has no arrow, *Professor* Winegarden, but may I ask, if time has no arrow, how come I live the past in my bookshop, in my books? In some real sense, the past is with me. And if I were a cleverer man, perhaps I could read the future there too ... But, you know, a humble second-hand bookseller, who am I to ask?'

'Thank you for an interesting question,' Jacob said, 'I shall have to ponder it.' He was silent for many seconds, pacing in front of the lectern. At last he said, 'I think the answer lies in the scaling up, from the little world of quantum effects to the big world of books and people ...'

'But is the soul in the big world, or the little?'

'Ah. That is the question ...'

'And either way, is it good for the Jews?'

A titter of laughter ran through the audience.

'Well of course, that is the *other* question!' said Winegarden, and the laughter became fuller, and relieved.

Afterwards his father said, 'Nice talk, Jake. Lovely. Not a word did I understand, but very nice. *Mazeltov, sh'koich,*' and he hugged tight his much taller son, a tear in his eye, patting his back and murmuring, 'My boy, my boy!' while Miriam looked on with studied patience.

Not long after the lecture, Winegarden was woken in the night. His father had had a stroke and was in hospital. Jacob went straight there and found his father lying in a sour-smelling ward, his bed hemmed in by metal bars. His kindly, much-loved, irritable father, uncomplicated bibliophile, complex man, was dying.

Harry murmured, 'That I should have to die in a cage, Jacob.'

'Shh, Dad, it's OK, it's a bed, it's not a cage, the bars are to stop you falling on the floor. It's OK.'

'OK? It's not OK. I'm dying, that's not OK. The nurses are like Aeroflot stewardesses. *Oi Gewalt.*'

Jacob smiled. 'You didn't like my lecture, fine, but this is a bit extreme, no?'

'Like it? I liked it. I just didn't understand it. The lack of understanding is killing me, *kein ayne'horah.*' He tried to laugh, and wheezed and put his hand to his chest.

Winegarden sat with his father through the night, holding his hand, as Harry had once held his.

***

Winegarden, now in his own hospital bed in the sallow, airless room, recalled this. The left side of his face drooped like overripe fruit. The remaining neuronal circuits of his brain fired at random, flashing on and off in all possible combinations, in parallel and in sequence. And, unsurprisingly, this induced moments of clarity. He thought, *'Die Entropie der Welt strebt einem Maximum zu.'* The entropy of the world tends to a maximum. Things run down, become destructured, disorganised.

How, he wondered, would he think of his stillborn boy, Joshua, had he lived? He imagined the stages of his life as a kind of thought experiment. Bad Bob Cohen – was he still around? – had told him a joke, and it came to his mind now. A bitter, Jewish, joke. Two men meeting on a train. Get lost! cries the first man before they've even had a chance to speak. Why so rude? asks the other fellow. Ach, because we would have got chatting, I have a daughter, you a son, perhaps we would have become friends, our children also, my daughter falls in love with your son, likely as not, marries him, then comes all the *tsuras*, they fall out, get divorced, lot of bitterness, we end up not speaking, so better not even start talking. Winegarden had liked the joke; the man on the train was like a thought-experimenter, one of Winegarden's own kind. He thought of Joshua: saved all the bitterness, disappointment, grief of living.

Thought experiments protect you, armour the vulnerable parts of your human heart. They can have significant effects in the real world. For good or ill. For ill: what if one could exterminate all the Jew vermin from the Reich? What if? Let's make it happen, a triumph of the will. A feat of breath-taking daring, of logistical genius, a wonder of social engineering on the grand scale. Winegarden shivered at the feeling that he had something in common with Nazis, the creative ability to conceive other worlds.

Father and absent son. Son and absent father. He felt alone with Joshua, a single parent unaccompanied. Alone with his dead son.

When Winegarden turned onto his back, his arm tangled in tubes and drips, and opened his eyes, Joshua was there, grinning at him. He fluctuated wildly in space-time. One instant he had a baby's big head with soft lips sputtering out bubbles of baby saliva. Then he was stroking a wispy black beard, his eyebrows sleek and black and thick as Jacob's once were before they went white and haywire. Then he was a stroppy adolescent, with a disrespectful expression.

Jacob loved him, but he was not sure he liked him.

'Had my barmitzvah?' said Josh, 'of course I've had my barmitzvah, you were there Dad. Don't you remember?'

'My remembering isn't so good these days, Josh.'

'Joshua.'

'Joshua. OK, so tell me. Fill me in.'

'Fill you in! That's a funny expression poo head, gaga-gaga-goo-goo. Yeah, whatever. What the f.... Actually the answer depends on the observer's location in space-time. As Einstein explained, gaga-goo-goo. Poo head.'

The lad seemed to fizzle and sputter in and out of existence, crackling with static. Hard to tell his age – fifteen, twenty? Or much older. But with a babyish face. Or young, but with an old face. He seemed short though for an adult, something half-finished.

Winegarden thought, Multiple universes. Scaling-up of quantum effects, entropy gaps. Josh – Joshua – might exist in other universes and now we're colliding, coinciding. Through small tears, wormholes in space-time, all that business. Or in memories, of things that did not happen as well as of things that did.

Joshua said, 'I remember when you gave your professorial inaugural lecture. I was four years old. What's an inorgial lepture Daddy? Why did that man do that funny laugh at his own joke Daddy? Grandpa was there, wasn't he? I remember, he shouted out things, he was funny!'

Winegarden wished to move around, to sit up, to get out of bed, but he seemed entrapped by steel bars to each side, like a farm gate, with an upright steel pole for the drip. What a sophisticated bed, he thought. Electrically operated, with integral folding safety sides for falls prevention, designed to manage risk, designed with smooth surfaces for infection control, designed for the convenience of nursing staff, with an intelligent profiling system and push-button manoeuvrability. Designed to detain the dying in life for pointless moments longer.

On Miriam's last visit, he'd tried to tell her about Joshua, about being reunited with his son. She'd said, 'I thought you didn't believe in the afterlife.'

'I do not. Afterlife, hah!'

'Well …'

'Miriam, my love, I was never apart from him, never. He is in me.'

She squeezed his hand, averting her face from him.

'And in you,' he insisted. 'You'd not admit it, but he is, he is.'

'Don't be silly, Jacob. I'm starting to worry about you.' She said it briskly but still would not look at him.

'My – son – came – to – see – me.'

She pressed his hand. 'All right, yes Jacob, darling, no doubt he did.'

Had Miriam really then said, *'He's not your son, not your son, you're not his father, you're not anybody's father, you don't have to feel bad. All those years I couldn't find the words, couldn't think of the right way to tell you …'*? Did she really say that? Probably not. Not in this universe at any rate.

'What – are you – trying to – t-t-e-ll – me?' It sounded like bbwww – mmm – gwww. Goo-goo-gaga.

'You're dribbling, darling.' She wiped away a bubble of saliva on his cracked lips, lips as thin as spiders' legs.

***

'Tell me about your barmitzvah, Josh.'

'Joshua. You interrupted my special day, shouted out something. At the reception. What's the going rate? Fifty quid, come on that's chicken feed. They're rolling in it, are mum's side of the family. Big house in Edgbaston. You interrupted, when I was telling an anecdote, me at thirteen, with down on my lip, not enough to shave, in front of all those people, all merry with the Kiddush wine and the whisky on the tables. I was telling them about you, about how mum went to see you play cricket, your slow bowling. Like Jim Laker you said. Like Bishen Bedi, like Chandrasekhar. Like Muralitharan. They were famous in your day. There was cheering when she got to the ground, you were bowling, they'd just slogged you for three sixes in an over and she thought the applause was for you. And you shouted out, "But I had him stumped next ball!" Stole my thunder. Steal your dead son's thunder. Hell's teeth, Dad.'

'Is that what happened?' Winegarden wondered. No, it can't be.

'At my wedding too. Shouted out, you did. Shouted, "Have you no shame, she's a scarlet woman, a shiksa!"'

'No I didn't.'

'You did, you did.'

'That's funny. My father did that to me. Exactly that to me at my wedding. Shouted out. After what he'd been through, I could understand. His wife, my mother, had just died. Your mum, she's never forgiven him.'

Josh wavered and shimmered in the overlit room, and faded from view. Winegarden thought, I, Jacob, the last of the Winegarden cell line, the only son of an only son, with not even an only son of my own.

But Josh was back. His head hung in the air, disembodied.

'So, what are you doing with yourself these days, Joshua? Is your job good?'

'Very good. Very stimulating. Big rush. Financial derivatives. Earn a bomb. Monte Carlo method.'

Winegarden now saw that his son was wearing a very sharp suit, he could make out the hand-stitching on the lapels. 'Nice schmutter,' he thought. That's what his father Harry would have said.

'Monte Carlo method? We use that in quantum physics. What's the maths?'

'The maths? Hell, Dad, where I work, no one understands the maths! It's something to do with statistics. You just apply the algorithm.'

Algorithm my foot, thought Winegarden. He said, 'Isn't that exactly what's led the world into this financial mess, Josh? Joshua.'

'You what?'

'Mess. Economic chaos, social disintegration. Like Weimar.'

'Weimar? What's Weimar?'

'Oh, for Heaven's sake.'

Josh really didn't know, the link had been broken, the past lost: all that was needed for history to repeat itself. Winegarden sighed. 'What I'm saying is, instability never did the Jews any good.'

'Ah, but nobody knows I'm a Jew. I'm not circumcised, remember!' said Joshua.

Jacob felt a cold rush in his chest. Of course the boy wasn't circumcised, he was stillborn.

'They blame the Jews, then look what happens ...'

'These days let them blame the Muslims,' replied Joshua, 'there's more of them.'

Jacob shook his head. 'You're not getting it.'

'No Dad, you're the one who's not getting it. Things move on. That's progress.'

Progress. One step further towards heat death, the flattening of the gradient. Maximum entropy.

'Make money while the sun shines, I say,' Josh continued. 'And while it's raining!'

What happened, wondered Winegarden, to all that parental influence, to those moral underpinnings, to the concept of being a mensch? Had it come to this?

Joshua said, 'You reacted against your father. I mean he was a bookseller, for Christ's sake. And a crusty old devil. Not even new books he sold. What life was ever saved by second-hand books ...?' – Josh's eyes had a malicious gleam to them – '... Or by thought experiments?'

Many, thought Winegarden, many lives. Yours included, Joshua. And mine. He said, 'What lives were saved by financial derivatives?'

'Fair point, dude. But I make money, money gives me choices.'

'What choices?'

'I could save lives if I chose.'

'Do you so choose?'

'No-o. But I could.'

Winegarden's son shimmered and looked up at him with big shiny dark eyes. He seemed too large for his short trousers.

'I want to be a famous pwofessor when I grow up, Daddy.'

Jacob smiled with parental pride. 'You'll have to work hard.'

'I will work hard, Daddy, if you'd like me to.'

Winegarden looked again. Now Joshua had gelled hair and a wolfish grin, and a moustache with waxed ends.

Jacob's wiry eyebrows twitched. 'Are you … homosexual?'

'No …'

'Because if you are, it's fine, many Jewish families have homosexual children, it's fine, we'll cope.'

'No Dad! No. I'm not gay.' Josh looked into the distance, thrust a thumb into his belt, planted his feet wide. 'Played the field, believe me, ladies' man through and through, know what I mean. Married out, weren't best pleased the pair of you. But it's only shiksas after all, go red as lobsters in the sun they do, the fair ones. But my God, those little tattoos just at the bottom of their back, the top of their bottom, what a come-on! Gets me every time. What Jewish girl would use that trick, eh?'

Josh paused for breath.

'Joshua, that's not how we brought you up, we never …'

His son interrupted him. 'My bucket list, right: make more money than any of my mates. Tick. Porsche 911-111. Tick. Marry a beautiful girl. Tick. Have my cake and eat it. Tick. Sleep with a woman for money. Fit and thick, Polish or Lithuanian, Teutonic, it's all good. Call it reparations. Fair trade of course. Fair in both senses! Can't say fairer than that, b-boom. Top of the range. Tick, tick, tick.'

Joshua was grinning at him. Winegarden shook his head.

'Only joking, Dad, only joking. Only j-o-k-i-n-g ...' His voice echoed slowly away into nothing.

Winegarden felt time pass. There was a steady pulse of machinery, flashing lights, the drip of fluid into tubes. His feeble hand felt for the bar of his cage. Things were winding down.

He heard a cough. He opened his eyes and his son stood there once more. Now he had curly sideburns and a long tangly black beard, and he wore a black homburg and a white shirt and black trousers, and little tassels of his tallith dangled down from under his shirt, giving him a dishevelled look.

'*Oi vei*! You were right, Dad, moral values I needed, a compass. So I'm training at the Yeshivah. Rabbi Guttmann recommended me. Gateshead. My accent is quite ... Tyneside, quite Geordie, Geordie-Jewish wye-aye.'

'I thought money was your God.'

'That was in another life, another universe. Now God is my God.'

'Lucky man.'

'Faith is not luck. You should have faith.'

'I cannot, how can I have faith when ...' Winegarden stopped himself from saying the bitter truth. That Joshua did not live. Instead he said, 'I am neither a believer nor a non-believer.'

Joshua snorted. 'What, not have your cake and not eat it either! The worst of all worlds.'

The worst of all universes.

Joshua's face shimmered and distorted.

'Have you visited your mother?'

Joshua looked thoughtful. 'My mother, she's quite narcissistic, isn't she.'

Winegarden prickled. 'I'm sorry? You're talking about the woman I've been married to for over forty years.'

'I'm only saying what you must have often thought, Dad. Don't tell me you haven't.' His face was serious, gone was the facetious mischief. 'You know ... She's in her own bubble, her space, she doesn't reach out, she never reached out to me.'

Winegarden thought, 'Like a baby stillborn, like a beast with his horn.'

He said, 'But she couldn't, could she, Joshua. You were the reason ...' He bit his tongue. 'You didn't answer my question. Have you been to see her?'

'Yes.'

'And?'

'She had lines on her face, not like I remembered.' Joshua shook his head and blinked. He stared straight ahead. 'I asked her to hold me but she scorned me and told me I was dead and could never return.'

'What! She said that?'

'Or words like it.' Joshua sighed. 'Hell, I don't know where I'm at.'

And he was smiling again, looking at his Rolex. He grasped Winegarden's emaciated hand in his.

'Long time no see, Dad, gotta go, give us a man hug!'

Jacob felt a little bubble of saliva burst with a soft pop on his lips. He formed another bubble, and another. Bwww-O-bwww-O-bwww. What if you drank a gallon of washing-up liquid and burped ...? Many bubbles, many, many! He'd closed his eyes in the soft warm embrace. When he opened them, Miriam was there, was it her? Lady Midnight. His eyes felt coated with Vaseline, everything was like a torn veil. Weary eyes.

I feel so alone, he thought.

'He was hugging his pillow,' said the nurse. She looked nothing like an Aeroflot stewardess.

'He doesn't know what he's doing,' said Miriam.

'I do know. Bww-O-bwww-O, bwgrwww.'

'Poor thing,' said the nurse, 'will you be all right with him?'

'Is he ...?'

The nurse nodded. 'I think so.'

Miriam took his hand. 'Try to sleep, Jacob darling.'

Winegarden felt weary in his brain and in his mangled heart, weary in his wasted, slack musculature, weary in his bones: bone-weary. Weary in his gaping turtle mouth. Weary. So weary.

And he felt his eyes look up to the left, to nothing, all by themselves, and felt his eyes close all by themselves, against the slowing pulse of the machines.

And, for all he knew, Miriam, still holding his hand, wept, all by herself ...

Acknowledgements

I'm very grateful to my fellow members of the Tindal Street Fiction Group for providing encouragement and constructive criticism as the novella developed: I owe them a huge debt of gratitude. Four members of the Tindal Street group read the novella in its entirety, and provided feedback: Gaynor Arnold, Al Beard, Mez Packer and Alan Mahar. Alan carried out a professional review of an early draft, providing invaluable advice that greatly strengthened the book. Mez has been a staunch friend and writing buddy for many years. Gaynor championed *Winegarden* from the beginning; I'm grateful for her support and for her careful editing of a short story which appeared in the collection edited by her and Julia Bell, *The Sea in Birmingham* (TSFG 2013). This story subsequently formed the starting point for the novella.

I'd like to thank Miles Larmour for his painstakingly detailed and very perceptive comments on three chapters, and Siân Miles for her generous encouragement and practical advice. My wife Diana Foster had the patience to listen to the whole book read aloud, and our sons Daniel and Joseph Ferner made helpful observations, particularly on the science. Other friends and family read one or more chapters – the list is not comprehensive, but includes the late France Brodeur, Robin Ferner, Rosalie Ferner, Celia Moss, Sue Shepherd and Becky Wylde.

Chapter 4, 'Lobster in the head', references Paul Durcan's poem, 'Golden mothers driving west'. Chapter 7, 'The entropy of the universe to a maximum climbs', quotes short phrases of Leonard Cohen's songs 'Bird on a wire' and 'Lady Midnight'. Finally, the set-up of the first part of Chapter 5, 'A Golem running on custard' – two men working on a problem in an isolated cottage, while the young daughter of one of them falls ill – pays indirect homage to the scenario of 'Los fabricantes de carbón' (usually translated as 'The charcoal burners'), a marvellous short story first published in 1918, by the Uruguayan writer Horacio Quiroga.

THE AUTHOR

Anthony Ferner was professor of international human resource management at De Montfort University and was head of research in the Faculty of Business and Law for 12 years. He retired in 2014. He has published many works of non-fiction, mainly about the behaviour of multinational companies.

His short story 'The Cat It Is That Dies' appeared in the anthology *The Sea In Birmingham*, edited by Gaynor Arnold and Julia Bell and published by Tindal Street Fiction Group in 2013. This story became the basis of *Winegarden*.

Another of Anthony Ferner's short stories, 'The tanks', was shortlisted for the Irish Times summer short story competition in 2014. He has also written drafts of three novels, and has been a member of the Tindal Street Fiction Group, based in Birmingham, since 2010.

More details are available from

www.hollandparkpress.co.uk/ferner

Holland Park Press is a unique publishing initiative. It gives contemporary Dutch writers the opportunity to be published in Dutch and English. We also publish new works written in English and translations of classic Dutch novels.

Visit www.hollandparkpress.co.uk for more information, and to visit our bookshop
http://hollandparkpress.co.uk/books.php

You can also follow us in the social media:

http://www.twitter.com/HollandParkPres
http://www.facebook.com/HollandParkPress
http://www.linkedin.com/company/holland-park-press
http://www.youtube.com/user/HollandParkPress